# Nancy Drew DIARIES™

*"When there's a mystery, I just can't help myself."*

*–Nancy Drew*

PAPERCUTZ™

# NANCY DREW DIARIES GRAPHIC NOVELS AVAILABLE FROM PAPERCUTZ

NANCY DREW DIARIES graphic novels are also available digitally wherever e-books are sold.

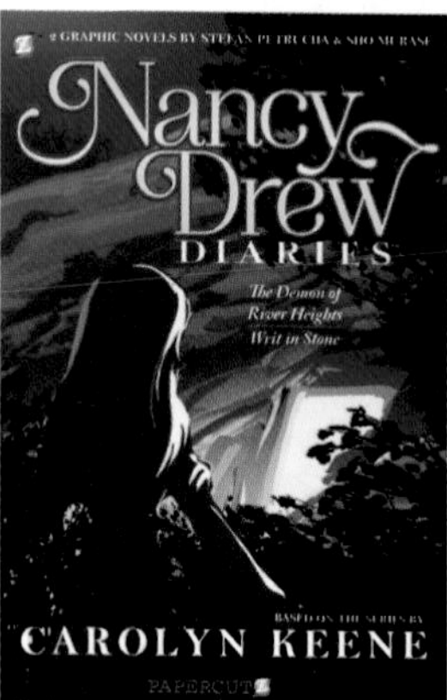

#1 "The Demon of River Heights" and "Writ in Stone"

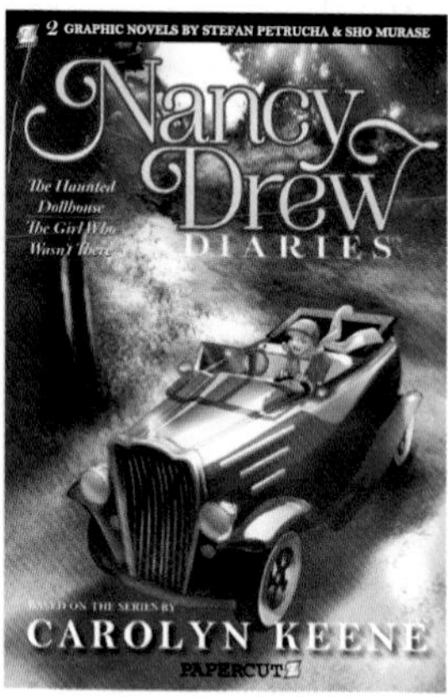

#2 "The Haunted Dollhouse" and "The Girl Who Wasn't There"

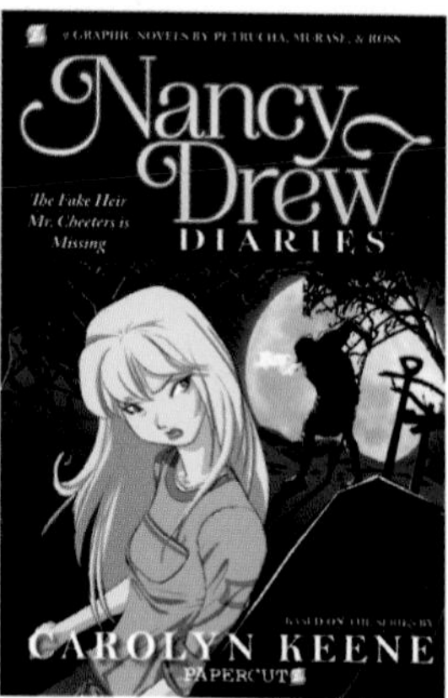

#3 "The Fake Heir" and "Mr Cheeters is Missing"

#4 "The Charmed Bracelet" and "Global Warning"

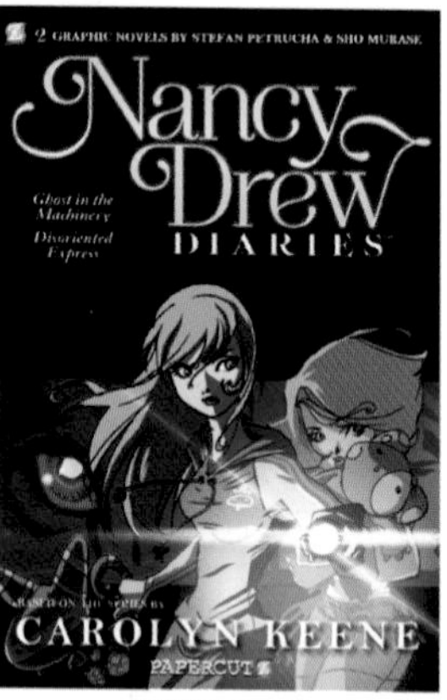

**COMING SOON!**
#5 "Ghost in the Machinery" and "The Disoriented Express"

**See page 175 for more NANCY DREW graphic novels!**

**NANCY DREW graphic novels are available at booksellers everywhere.**

NANCY DREW DIARIES graphic novels are $9.99 each and available only in paperback. You may also order online at www.papercutz.com. Or call 1-800-886-1223, Monday through Friday, 9 – 5 EST. MC, Visa, and AmEx accepted. To order by mail, please add $4.00 for postage and handling for first book ordered, $1.00 for each additional book and make check payable to NBM Publishing.

Send to: Papercutz, 160 Broadway, Suite 700, East Wing, New York, NY 10038.

**papercutz.com**

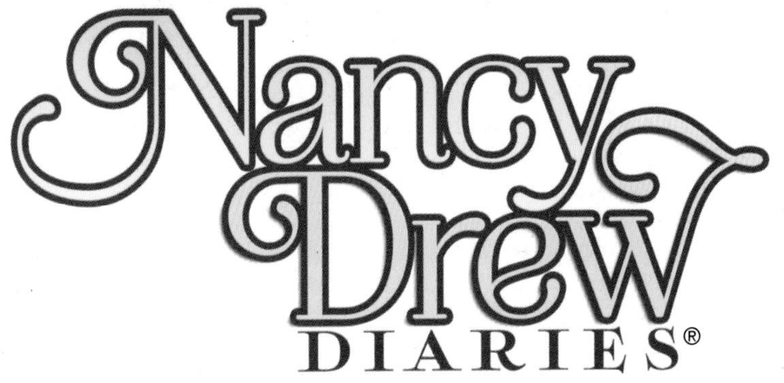


# #4 "The Charmed Bracelet" and "Global Warning"

Based on the series by
CAROLYN KEENE
STEFAN PETRUCHA • Writer
DANIEL VAUGHN ROSS and SHO MURASE • Artists
with 3D CG elements by LUIS LUNDGREN
and CARLOS JOSE GUZMAN

PAPERCUTZ™
New York

Nancy Drew Diaries
#4

"The Charmed Bracelet" and "Global Warning"
STEFAN PETRUCHA – Writer
DANIEL VAUGHN ROSS – Artist, "The Charmed Bracelet"
SHO MURASE – Artist, "Global Warning"
with 3D CG elements by LUIS LUNDGREN ("The Charmed Bracelet")
and CARLOS JOSE GUZMAN ("Global Warning")
BRYAN SENKA – Letterer
CARLOS JOSE GUZMAN – Colorist
NOAH SHARMA – Editorial Intern
JEFF WHITMAN – Production Coordinator
MICHAEL PETRANEK – Associate Editor
JIM SALICRUP – Original Editor
BETH SCORZATO – Editor
JIM SALICRUP
Editor-in-Chief

ISBN: 978-1-62991-158-8


Originally published as NANCY DREW Girl Detective #7 and #8.
Published by arrangement with Aladdin Paperbacks,
an imprint of Simon & Schuster Children's Publishing Division.

Printed in South Korea
January 2015 by We SP Corp.
2F, 507-8 Munbal-dong, Gyoha-eup
Paju City, Gyunggi-do
Seoul, Gyeonggi-do 413-756

Distributed by Macmillian
First Printing

NANCY DREW HERE, WITH LAWYER-DAD, CARSON. HE REPRESENTS THE INSURANCE COMPANY FOR THE BIGGEST COMPANY HERE IN RIVER HEIGHTS, COMPUTER CHIP MAKER RACKHAM INDUSTRIES.
THEY EMPLOY MOST OF THE PEOPLE IN TOWN, SO YOU'D THINK THEY'D BE MORE VISITOR-FRIENDLY.
NOPE! SECURITY HERE MAKES THE PENTAGON IN WASHINGTON D.C. LOOK WARM AND FUZZY.
CHAPTER ONE: TINY CHIP, BIG MESS

DAD WAS INVITED TO TOUR -- JUST TO MAKE SURE EVERYTHING WAS SHIP-SHAPE.
VRRRRRR
I'D NEVER BEEN INSIDE, AND WHAT GIRL DETECTIVE WOULDN'T BE CURIOUS? SO HE LET ME TAG ALONG.

THE PLACE WAS TIGHT AS A DRUM. YOU COULDN'T GET IN *OR* OUT WITHOUT BEING PHOTOGRAPHED.
CLICK
CLICK

VISITOR
GLAD I WASN'T PICKING MY NOSE.

A MAZE OF FANCY OFFICES AND BORING EXECS FINALLY LED US TO LARS JENSEN, AN *INVENTOR* WHO PROMISED TO SHOW US SOMETHING MORE INTERESTING.
IT'S VERY EXCITING! WE'VE JUST COMPLETED THE PROTOTYPE FOR A SUPER-SMALL TITANIUM CHIP THAT CAN PROCESS A THOUSAND TIMES MORE DATA THAN CHIPS TWICE ITS SIZE!
HOLD THIS PLEASE, MS. DREW? I NEED *BOTH* HANDS TO GET THE DOOR OPEN.
IT HAS TO SCAN MY HAND *WHILE* I ENTER THE CODE.
AUTHORIZED PERSONNEL ONLY
GEE, WHAT DO YOU DO WHEN YOU'RE *ALONE*?
HA! I STAY *THIRSTY*!
ALL THIS SECURITY MAY LIMIT SNACKING, BUT IT MAKES STEALING THE CHIP, WELL, *VIRTUALLY*...

IMPOSSIBLE?!
WELL, AS THEY SAY, I GUESS
NOTHING IS IMPOSSIBLE!

MARGO! THE CHIP... IT'S MISSING!
THAT'S *IMPOSSIBLE!*
THAT'S WHAT *I* SAID!
HOW LONG HAVE YOU BEEN GONE?!
ONLY FIFTEEN MINUTES!
WE'VE GOT TO RECOVER THE CHIP FAST! OUTSIDE THIS CONTROLLED ENVIRONMENT ITS RARE METALS WILL *CORRODE* IN A WEEK! THE PROJECT WILL BE BACK TO SQUARE ONE!
IT'D COST A *FORTUNE!* WE'D HAVE TO LAY OFF MOST OF THE PEOPLE IN YOUR DEPARTMENT!

IS THAT THE CHIP?
THE REAL THING IS MUCH SMALLER, OF COURSE.
I'M CHECKING THE SECURITY CAMERAS. THEY SHOULD SHOW US WHAT HAPPENED.
GASP THEY WERE DISABLED AT 10:02!
THAT'S 12 MINUTES AGO, RIGHT AFTER YOU LEFT--

OW!
NANCY GETS PRETTY SINGLE-MINDED ABOUT A MYSTERY! IT CAN MAKE HER FORGET, WELL, EVERYTHING ELSE.

SORRY! I'LL CLEAN UP IN THE LADIES ROOM.

IT'S TRUE, I COULD BE ABSENT-MINDED WHILE SOLVING A MYSTERY, BUT THAT SPILL WAS ON PURPOSE! I WANTED TO SNIFF ABOUT *ALONE* FOR CLUES WHILE THE SCENT WAS STILL STRONG...AND MAYBE GET A DONUT.
SEEMS TO BE A DAY FOR *DISASTERS*. MY NAME'S PETER, BY THE WAY. PETER BRAVERMAN.

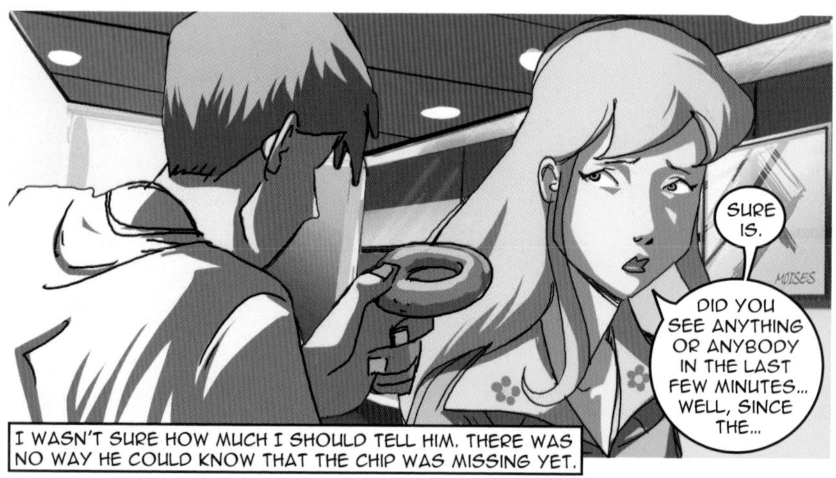
SURE IS.
DID YOU SEE ANYTHING OR ANYBODY IN THE LAST FEW MINUTES... WELL, SINCE THE...
I WASN'T SURE HOW MUCH I SHOULD TELL HIM. THERE WAS NO WAY HE COULD KNOW THAT THE CHIP WAS MISSING YET.
MOISES

YOU MEAN SINCE THAT FANCY CHIP GOT *SWIPED*?!
MOISES

YOU KNOW ABOUT THAT?
I SEE THINGS. I HEAR THINGS.

"LIKE I KNOW, FOR INSTANCE, THAT SOME JEALOUS EXECS THINK THE CHIP IS TOO RISKY AND EXPENSIVE. THEY'D *LOVE* TO SEE THE PROJECT JUST GO AWAY."
SORRY, LARS...
"THAT CHIP SUCKED UP ALL THE MONEY THAT COULD BE GOING TO *THEIR* PROJECTS."

SORRY, WALTER.
WALTER REACH
PROJECT 5
NO FUNDING

"NOT ONLY THAT, THEY WERE SHUT OUT OF THE DECISION-MAKING PROCESS FOR COMPLAINING."
"I THINK YOU'LL FIND A *FEW* PEOPLE HERE WHO'LL BE HAPPY THAT CHIP IS GONE!"

SO, WHOM SPECIFICALLY ARE WE TALKING ABOUT?
WALTER REACH FOR ONE. SAY, HAVE YOU BEEN TO AREA 5 WHERE HE HAS HIS PROJECTS?

AFTER THAT, NATURALLY, I FIGURED I'D CHECK OUT AREA 5.
I WAS SURPRISED HOW EASY IT WAS TO REACH. IT DIDN'T HAVE ANY OF THE HIGH TECH PRECAUTIONS MR. JENKINS' LAB DID.

IT LOOKED LIKE IT WOULD BE EASY TO JUST WALK ON IN.

BUT APPEARANCES CAN BE *DECEIVING!*

HEY!

GASP!

I COULD TELL FROM HIS ID BADGE THAT THIS WAS WALTER REACH. PETER WAS RIGHT. HE WAS DEFINITELY THE *DISGRUNTLED* TYPE.

WHO THE *HECK* ARE YOU? WHAT ARE YOU *DOING* HERE?!

UH... I WAS JUST--

SEE, I'M SORT OF KNOWN AS AN AMATEUR DETECTIVE AND I WAS JUST TRYING TO HELP--
I DON'T CARE WHO YOU ARE! YOU'RE NOT AUTHORIZED TO BE IN THAT AREA! I SHOULD HAVE YOU ARRESTED.
PETER DIDN'T SEEM TERRIBLY SHOCKED OR UPSET ABOUT MY BEING IN TROUBLE.
SORRY, NANCY. STAY IN TOUCH.
DAD SEEMED A LITTLE TOO AMUSED BY THE WHOLE THING.
I HAVE TO WAIT HERE FOR THE INSURANCE REP TO COME...
...BUT, MR. REACH SAID HE WILL NOT HAVE YOU ARRESTED, IF YOU GO QUIETLY.

KEEP UP THE GOOD WORK.
I WASN'T BEING **RUDE**. THE SECURITY REALLY **WAS** AMAZING.
SO HOW DID SOMEONE STEAL THE CHIP?

I **HATED** LEAVING JUST WHEN THINGS WERE GETTING INTERESTING, SO I TOOK MY TIME ON THE WAY OUT TO CHECK OUT THE BUILDING.
MISS, I'LL HAVE TO ASK YOU TO LEAVE THE PREMISES.
I GUESS THE SHADOW LOOKING DOWN AT ME **COULD** HAVE BEEN SOME EXEC ENJOYING HIS OFFICE VIEW...

...OR WALTER REACH MAKING SURE I LEFT.
WHAT KIND OF **THREAT** DID HE THINK I WAS, ANYWAY?!

DID REACH REALLY THINK I WAS A *SPY* FOR A RIVAL COMPANY OR WAS HE HIDING SOMETHING *ELSE*?

BUT, IF THE DAY WASN'T STRANGE ENOUGH ALREADY, IT WAS ABOUT TO GET EVEN STRANGER!

*CHIEF McGINNIS'S* SQUAD CAR WAS OUTSIDE THE CAMERA STORE WHERE MY BOYFRIEND NED AND I HAD BROWSED JUST THE DAY BEFORE.
Crazy Carls Cameras
Sale

RIVER HEIGHTS HAS MORE THAN ITS SHARE OF CRIME, BUT A COP CAR IN FRONT OF ANY STORE IS STILL A BIT ***UNUSUAL***.

Crazy Carl's Cameras

SO, OF ***COURSE***, I HAD TO CHECK IT OUT.

FUNNY, I'D ADMIRED A LITTLE CAMERA HERE THE DAY BEFORE, BUT HADN'T BOUGHT IT.

I WASN'T SURE ***WHAT*** I'D FIND TODAY, BUT I SURE DIDN'T EXPECT TO SEE...

NANCY! WILL YOU PLEASE TELL CHIEF McGINNIS I'M INNOCENT? MAYBE HE'LL BELIEVE YOU THAT I'D NEVER SHOPLIFT!
SHOP-LIFT?!

MY BOYFRIEND, NED'S A LOT OF THINGS, MOSTLY WONDERFUL THINGS, BUT THIEF WAS DEFINITELY NOT ON THE LIST -- AND CHIEF McGINNIS KNEW IT.
THIS MUST BE SOME KIND OF A JOKE. AND ARE THOSE HANDCUFFS REALLY NECESSARY?!

I SUPPOSE NOT, NANCY, BUT THIS IS NO JOKE!
I WAS AS SURPRISED AS YOU WHEN I GO THE CALL, BUT THERE'S THIS ONE SIMPLE FACT...

HE HAD THIS IN HIS POCKET.
GASP!
HMM. YOU ACT LIKE YOU'VE SEEN IT BEFORE.
ACTUALLY, I HAD!
WANT TO TELL ME ABOUT IT?
I... I... UH...
HOW COULD I TELL CHIEF McGINNIS IT WAS THE VERY SAME TINY SPY CAMERA NED SAW ME ADMIRE THE DAY BEFORE?

GO ON AND TELL HIM, NANCY!
I'VE GOT NOTHING TO HIDE, AND I CERTAINLY DON'T WANT YOU TO LIE!
AND, WHY WOULD YOU LIE UNLESS YOU THOUGHT THERE WAS SOME CHANCE I STOLE IT?
I'D NEVER THINK THAT, NED! I WAS JUST... SURPRISED!
IT WAS TRUE. BUT SOMEHOW, I DON'T THINK NED FOUND ANY COMFORT IN MY EXPLANATION.
I HATE TO BREAK UP YOUR LITTLE QUARREL, BUT I HAVE A JOB TO DO HERE.

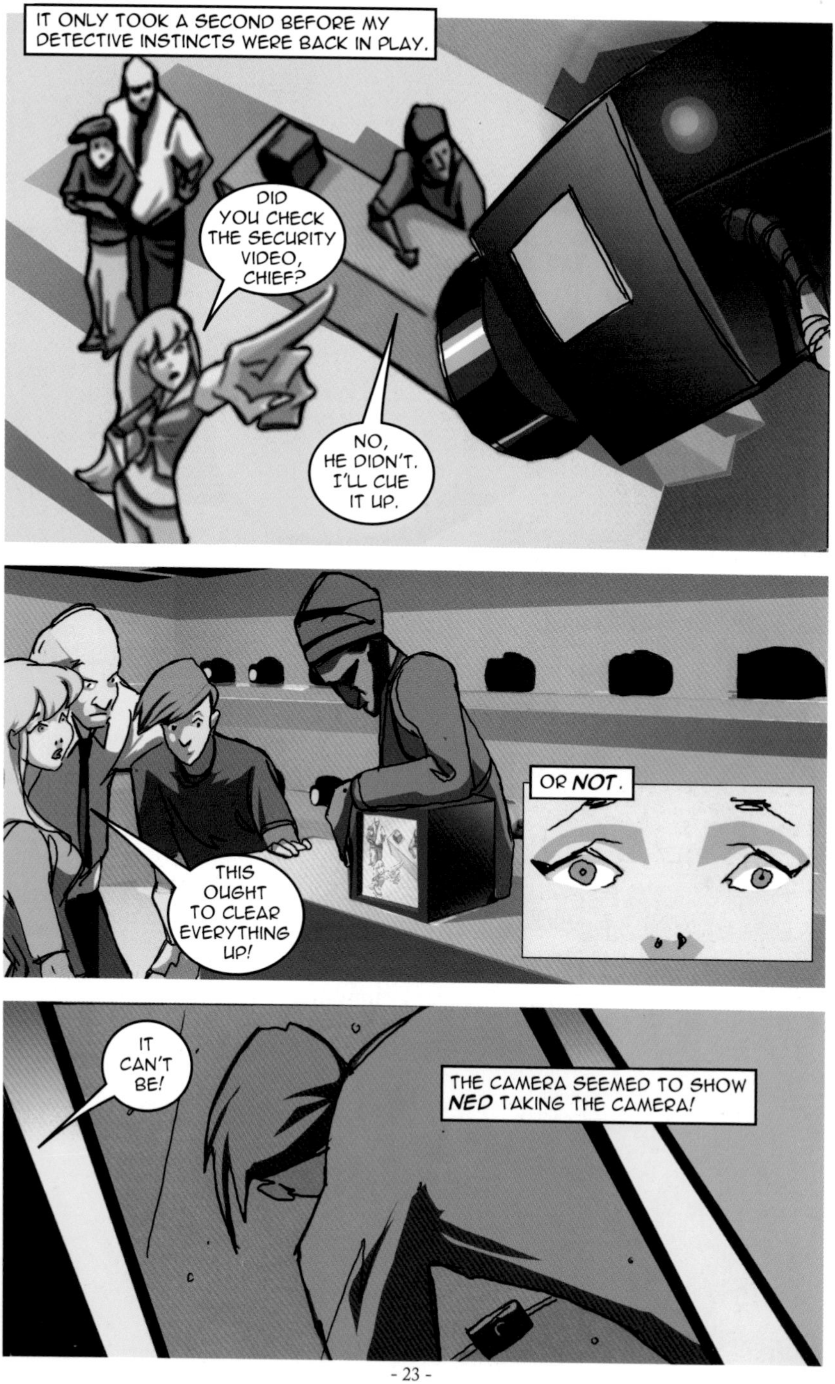

IT ONLY TOOK A SECOND BEFORE MY DETECTIVE INSTINCTS WERE BACK IN PLAY.

DID YOU CHECK THE SECURITY VIDEO, CHIEF?

NO, HE DIDN'T. I'LL CUE IT UP.

THAT COULD BE ANYONE ON THAT TAPE -- EXCEPT NED!
THAT REAL SHOPLIFTER MUST HAVE PANICKED AND SLIPPED THE CAMERA INTO NED'S POCKET!
KAREEM, YOU DID GET THE CAMERA BACK AND NED HAS NO PRIOR RECORD. ANY CHANCE YOU'LL SPARE ME THE PAPER WORK AND NOT PRESS CHARGES?!
NO CHANCE!
YOU KNOW HOW MUCH I LOSE TO THIEVES? I WANT HIM TO BE AN EXAMPLE!
C'MON, NED. I HAVE TO TAKE YOU TO THE STATION AND BOOK YOU.
THIS HAS TO BE A JOKE! CHIEF, IT'S NED!
NO ONE'S LAUGHING, NANCY! PICK HIM UP IN ABOUT AN HOUR. THE HEARING WILL BE NEXT WEEK.
Cameras

AFTER THE BOOKING, NED WAS SO UPSET HE BARELY SPOKE.
THE NEXT DAY, I ASKED HIM TO COME FOR LUNCH AND LISTEN TO SOME OF MY DAD'S EXPERT LEGAL ADVICE.
WHILE I WAS WAITING, I CHECKED THE MAIL.

THERE WAS A PACKAGE FOR ME. I WONDERED IF IT WAS MY BIRTHDAY AND I'D JUST FORGOTTEN, AGAIN. BUT THERE WAS NO RETURN ADDRESS.

INSIDE WAS A CHARM BRACELET WITH NO CARD.
NOW WHO--

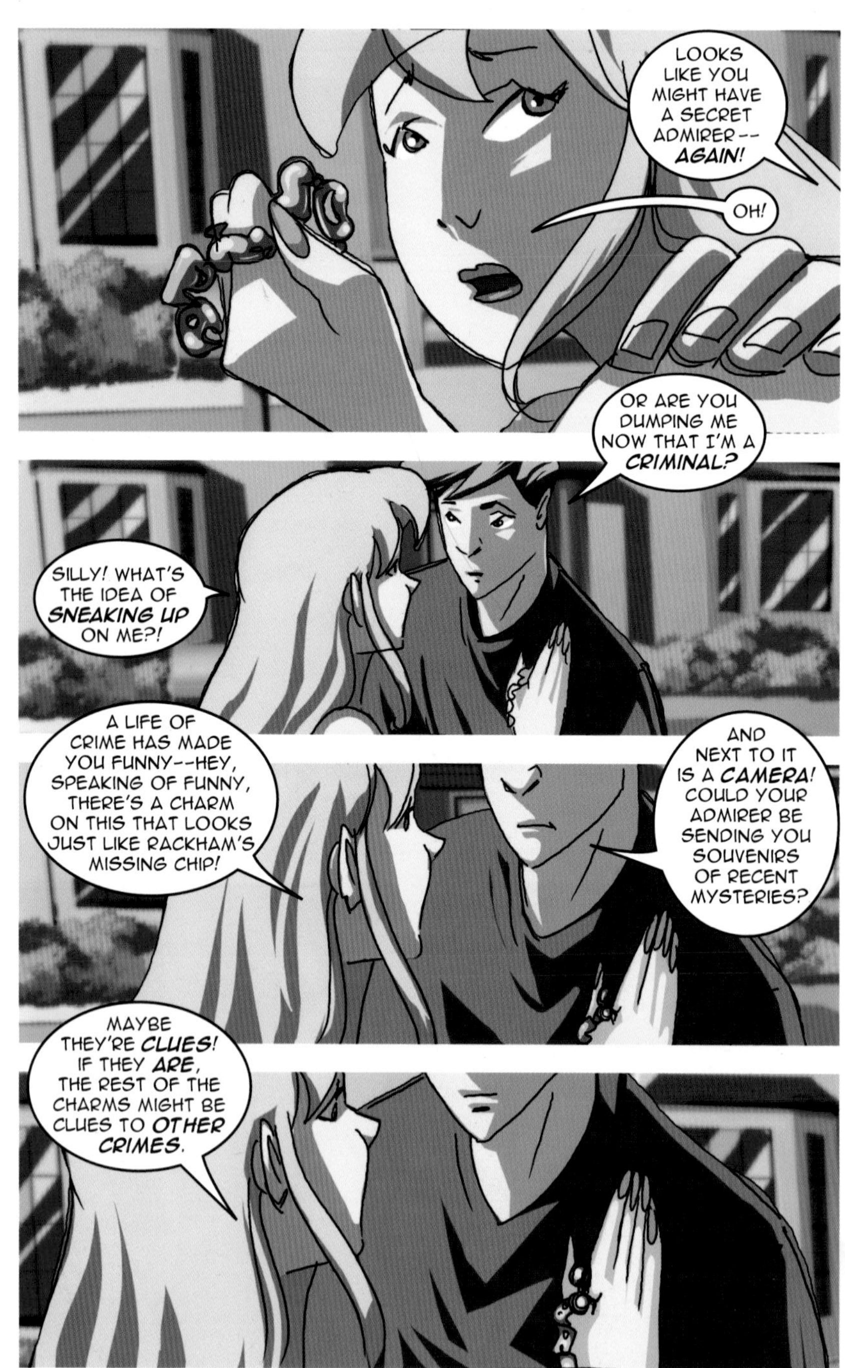
LOOKS LIKE YOU MIGHT HAVE A SECRET ADMIRER-- AGAIN!
OH!
OR ARE YOU DUMPING ME NOW THAT I'M A CRIMINAL?
SILLY! WHAT'S THE IDEA OF SNEAKING UP ON ME?!
A LIFE OF CRIME HAS MADE YOU FUNNY--HEY, SPEAKING OF FUNNY, THERE'S A CHARM ON THIS THAT LOOKS JUST LIKE RACKHAM'S MISSING CHIP!
AND NEXT TO IT IS A CAMERA! COULD YOUR ADMIRER BE SENDING YOU SOUVENIRS OF RECENT MYSTERIES?
MAYBE THEY'RE CLUES! IF THEY ARE, THE REST OF THE CHARMS MIGHT BE CLUES TO OTHER CRIMES.

THE NEW MYSTERY TOOK NED'S MIND OFF HIS LEGAL PROBLEMS, SO IT WAS EASY TO TALK HIM INTO A VISIT TO RIVER HEIGHTS CLASSIC AND CUSTOM MOTORCYCLE SHOP TO LEARN MORE ABOUT THE NEXT CHARM.
Classic and Custom
Motorcycle Shop

CAN YOU TELL ME WHAT KIND OF MOTORCYCLE THIS IS?
HMM. A VERY SMALL ONE?

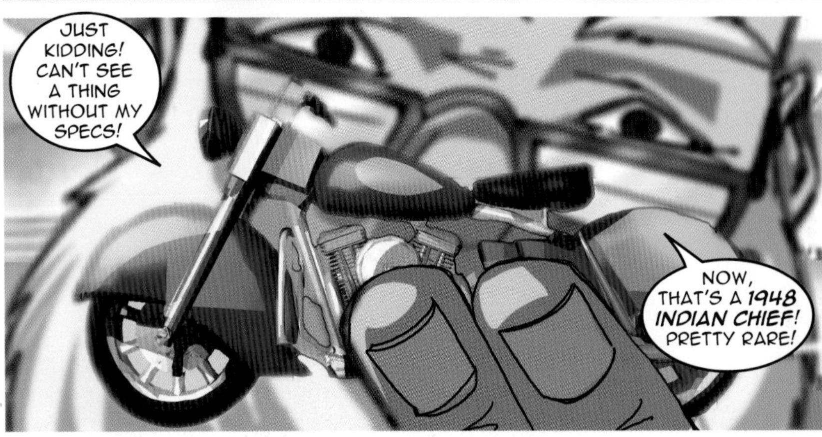
JUST KIDDING! CAN'T SEE A THING WITHOUT MY SPECS!
NOW, THAT'S A 1948 INDIAN CHIEF! PRETTY RARE!

VERY FEW OF THESE BEAUTIES STILL AROUND.
BY AN AMAZING **COINCIDENCE** WE HAVE ONE RIGHT OVER HERE...
YOU MEAN THE ONE BEING **STOLEN** BY THAT MASKED MAN?

HEY, ***YOU***! GET OFF THAT...
SPLUTTER
VROOOOM
PUTT
PUTT
PUTT

NANCE, LOOK OUT!

VROOOM

VROOOM

THE HIGH HORSEPOWER THIEF WAS HEADED RIGHT FOR ME!
VROOOOM

USUALLY, I'D BE WONDERING IF I KNEW HIM OR *WHY* HE WAS TRYING TO KILL ME.
VROOOM

I'VE GOT YOU, NANCY!

BUT THERE REALLY WASN'T *TIME*!

VROOOM

LOOK OUT!
END CHAPTER ONE

NOT SO GOOD FOR THE ***THIEF*** RIDING THE CLASSIC MOTORCYCLE!

CRAAASHH

VROOOM

# CHAPTER TWO: ADRENALINE RUSH

YOU OKAY?
UNNGH! SORT OF!
I THINK I HIT MY HEAD ON THE CARBURETOR OF THAT MOTO GUZZI.
YOU'VE GOT A CUT! THIS REALLY ISN'T YOUR DAY!
BETTER THAT THAN TIRE TRACKS, LADY!
THAT THIEF COULD'VE KILLED HIM IF YOU HADN'T PULLED HIM TO SAFETY!
THE CUT ISN'T SO BAD, BUT YOU GOT A REAL BUMP!
I'M FINE! I'LL DO IT.
...YES, OFFICER, THAT'S RIVER HEIGHTS CLASSIC BIKE SHOP...

I DON'T KNOW WHAT THAT **NUT** WAS THINKIN'! THE GUY DIDN'T EVEN KNOW HOW TO **RIDE** IT!

River Heights Classic and Custom Motorcycle Shop

WHOEVER IT WAS MUST HAVE PLANNED THIS HEIST **BEFORE** HE PUT THE MOTORCYCLE CHARM ON THAT BRACELET.

I EXPECT TO FIND NANCY WHEREVER THERE'S TROUBLE, NED, BUT THIS IS ALSO THE SECOND ROBBERY **YOU'RE** AT THIS WEEK!

I THOUGHT MAYBE IT WAS THE BRUISE, SO AT SUSIE'S WE GOT SOME ICE.
I MAY BE GOOD WITH CRIME, BUT I DIDN'T EVEN REALIZE THAT POOR NED'S EGO COULD USE AN ICE PACK, TOO!
I DON'T CARE IF NED IS A CROOK! IT'S NANCY WHO GETS HIM INTO TROUBLE.
WHY, I HEAR SHE ALMOST GOT HIM KILLED TODAY!
DEIDRE AND HER BOYFRIEND-OF-THE-DAY WEREN'T HELPING!

NO, NO, SHE *SAVED* THE KLEPTOMANIAC'S LIFE!

UH-OH. WHAT ARE WE WALKING INTO?

LIFE OF *CRIME*, I SHOULD SAY! I HEARD THE BUST OF ALEXANDER HAMILTON WAS STOLEN FROM THE LOBBY OF THE HAMILTON ARMS!

THEN AGAIN, NED NICKERSON COULDN'T BE *THAT* BOLD! I FIGURE HE'S ONLY GOOD FOR RUNNING *AWAY* FROM MOTORCYCLES!

DON'T WORRY, NED! ANYONE WHO *KNOWS* YOU COULDN'T POSSIBLY BELIEVE YOU'RE A KLEPTOMANIAC.

AND ANYONE WHO *DOESN'T* KNOW YOU, KNOWS KLEPTOMANIA IS A *SICKNESS* AND YOU CAN'T *HELP* YOURSELF.

EVER HAVE ONE OF THOSE DAYS WHEN PEOPLE JUST KEEP SAYING THE *WRONG* THINGS?!

THAT'S IT, I'M GOING HOME!
I'LL DRIVE YOU.

THANKS, BUT I THINK I'VE HAD ENOUGH HELP TODAY!
IT WAS THEN I FINALLY REALIZED THAT AFTER BEING ARRESTED YESTERDAY, MY SAVING HIM INSTEAD OF THE OTHER WAY AROUND, WASN'T SITTING WELL.

IT WAS LIKE HE WAS LOOKING FOR A WAY TO BE THE GOOD GUY HE IS, BUT NO ONE WAS GIVING HIM A CHANCE.
NICE GOING, BESS! NED GETS ARRESTED, MISTAKEN FOR A MOTOCROSS TRACK AND NOW HE'S SUPPOSED TO BE RELIEVED IF PEOPLE THINK HE'S A KLEPTO?

I WISH I COULD COMFORT HIM. I JUST DON'T KNOW WHAT TO SAY.
I JUST CAN'T WRAP MY HEAD AROUND THE IDEA THAT ANYONE WOULD THINK NED'S A THIEF.

I HAVE TO CATCH THAT CRAZY THIEF BEFORE SOMETHING ELSE HAPPENS TO NED.

THAT BRACELET IS LIKE A TROPHY CASE. WHOEVER THE CROOK IS, HE'S A HEAD CASE, ALL RIGHT!

EXACTLY! SO, **DON'T** WORRY, NANCY!

THE CHIEF KNOWS NED DOESN'T FIT THE **PROFILE** FOR A KLEPTO. IT'LL ALL WORK OUT.

PROFILE FOR A KLEPTO! OF COURSE!

GEORGE, WHERE'S YOUR **LAPTOP**?

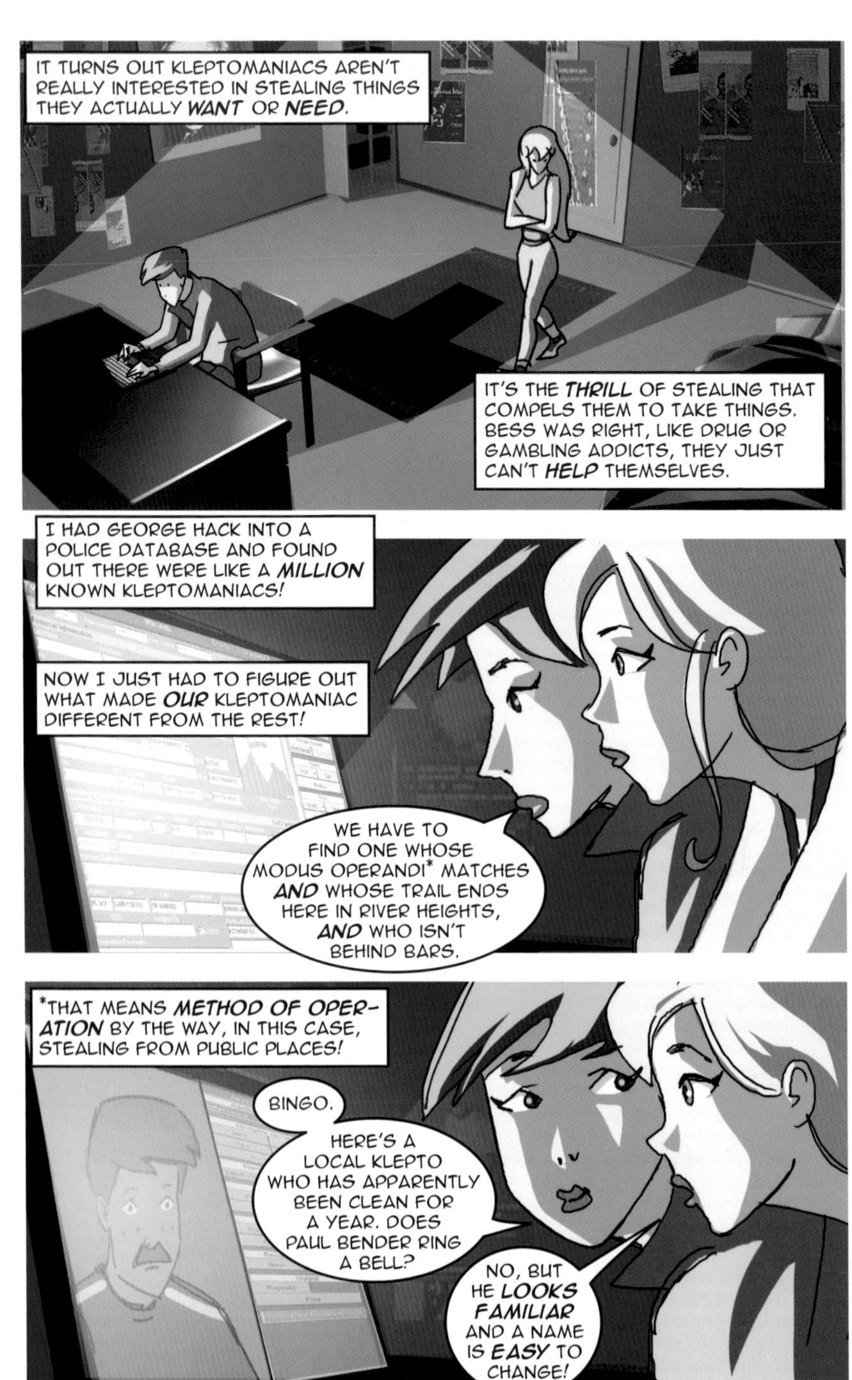
IT TURNS OUT KLEPTOMANIACS AREN'T REALLY INTERESTED IN STEALING THINGS THEY ACTUALLY WANT OR NEED.
IT'S THE THRILL OF STEALING THAT COMPELS THEM TO TAKE THINGS. BESS WAS RIGHT, LIKE DRUG OR GAMBLING ADDICTS, THEY JUST CAN'T HELP THEMSELVES.
I HAD GEORGE HACK INTO A POLICE DATABASE AND FOUND OUT THERE WERE LIKE A MILLION KNOWN KLEPTOMANIACS!
NOW I JUST HAD TO FIGURE OUT WHAT MADE OUR KLEPTOMANIAC DIFFERENT FROM THE REST!
WE HAVE TO FIND ONE WHOSE MODUS OPERANDI* MATCHES AND WHOSE TRAIL ENDS HERE IN RIVER HEIGHTS, AND WHO ISN'T BEHIND BARS.
*THAT MEANS METHOD OF OPERATION BY THE WAY, IN THIS CASE, STEALING FROM PUBLIC PLACES!
BINGO.
HERE'S A LOCAL KLEPTO WHO HAS APPARENTLY BEEN CLEAN FOR A YEAR. DOES PAUL BENDER RING A BELL?
NO, BUT HE LOOKS FAMILIAR AND A NAME IS EASY TO CHANGE!

NOT ONLY THAT, I FIGURED OUR KLEPTO HAD TO BE *WORKING* FOR RACKHAM! HOW *ELSE* COULD HE BE ABLE TO GET IN AND STEAL THAT CHIP?!
THAT MEANT WE HAD TO SEARCH THEIR *EMPLOYEE FILES*. BUT, WHILE GEORGE HAD AN EASY TIME GETTING INTO POLICE DATABASES...
NO PARKIN
RACKHAM'S COMPUTER FILES WERE *REALLY* PROTECTED, WHICH MEANT WE HAD TO GET A LOT *CLOSER*!

SO, BESS, YOU'RE *SURE* YOU WANT TO DO THIS? IT COULD BE *DANGER-OUS*.
I THINK I CAN DISTRACT ONE *CUTE* SECURITY GUARD WITHOUT *TOO* MUCH SUFFERING.

VISITORS AT THIS HOUR?!
RENTA
COP

GEORGE AND I DID OUR CAT BURGLAR THING AND TRIED TO MAKE OURSELVES INVISIBLE...

AFTER ***SABOTAGING*** SOME WIRES ON HER CAR, BESS DID HER BEST IMITATION OF A HELPLESS FEMALE.

EXCUSE, ME, SIR! I WONDER IF YOU CAN HELP ME! IT'S MY ***CAR***...

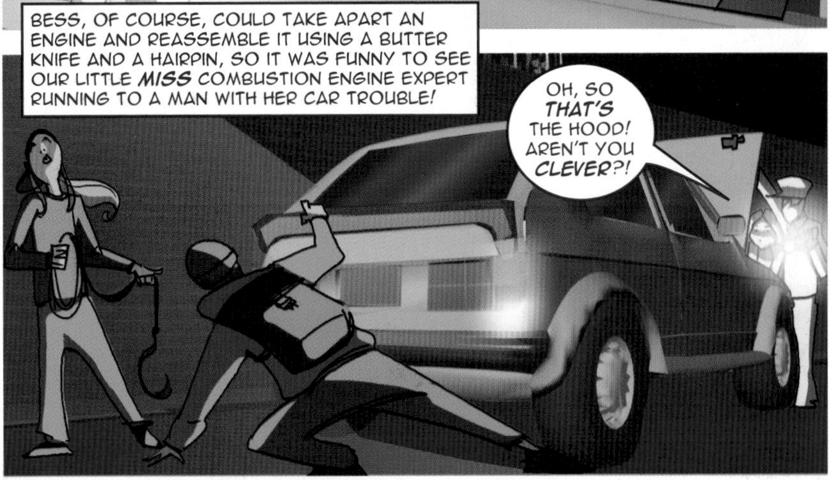

BESS, OF COURSE, COULD TAKE APART AN ENGINE AND REASSEMBLE IT USING A BUTTER KNIFE AND A HAIRPIN, SO IT WAS FUNNY TO SEE OUR LITTLE ***MISS*** COMBUSTION ENGINE EXPERT RUNNING TO A MAN WITH HER CAR TROUBLE!

OH, SO ***THAT'S*** THE HOOD! AREN'T YOU ***CLEVER***?!

THIS PLACE WAS LOCKED-UP TIGHTER THAN FORT KNOX, BUT THE DAY I WAS ASKED TO LEAVE, I HAD NOTICED ONE WAY IN.
THE BUILDING HAD A BASEMENT VENTILATION FAN, PROBABLY FOR LETTING OUT MOISTURE AS WELL AS A TOXIC NATURAL GAS CALLED RADON.
AND I KNEW THAT THE THIEF HADN'T USED IT.

THE CRIME HAD OCCURRED ON A WEEKDAY IN BROAD DAYLIGHT, WITH EVERYONE WATCHING.
BUT, IT WAS ALSO JUST THE THING FOR LETTING IN AMATEUR DETECTIVES.

SO, THIS WAS DEFINITELY AN INSIDE JOB. I WAS SO SURE, I WAS WILLING TO BET RACKHAM WOULDN'T PRESS CHARGES AGAINST US IF WE WERE CAUGHT!

I COULDN'T JUST ASK FOR ACCESS, THOUGH! THE THIEF COULD BE ANYONE WALKING THE HALLWAYS OF RACKHAM INDUSTRY HEADQUARTERS...

... FROM THE ADMINISTRATIVE ASSISTANTS TO THE CEO!

THE ONLY OTHER THING I KNEW ABOUT HIM WAS THAT HE SENT ME THE CHARM BRACELET.

BUT, WHY ME?!

INTER-SECTION! WHICH WAY?!

THAT WAY.
I HEAR HUMMING. IT'S PROBABLY THE HEATING AND VENTING UNITS.

MEANWHILE, BESS WAS DOING HER BEST TO MAKE THE SECURITY GUARD BELIEVE THAT HE KNEW MORE ABOUT CARS THAN SHE DID!
I AM SO LUCKY YOU WERE HERE!

SO, THAT FZZZT I HEARD RIGHT BEFORE IT DIED MIGHT HAVE BEEN THIS WIRE?
MAYBE. OR YOU MAY HAVE TO REPLACE THE DISTRIBUTOR. I CAN CALL THE GARAGE FOR YOU.

OH, BUT, IT'S SO LATE AND YOU SEEM AWFULLY SMART ABOUT THESE THINGS. DON'T YOU THINK YOU COULD TRY TO, WELL, RECONNECT THE THINGAMAJIG TO THE WHATSITS?
I SUPPOSE!

THE DUCT LED US INTO THE BASEMENT.
THWUNK

WE WERE ***IN***, BUT WE STILL HAD TO FIND THE COMPUTER WITH THE EMPLOYEE DATABASE!
WE'VE GOT TO FIND THE HUMAN RESOURCES OFFICE.
WELL, I KNOW IT ISN'T IN THE BASE-MENT!

IT'S ON THE FIRST FLOOR, NEAR THE LOBBY. I REMEMBER FROM THE TOUR. THERE'S THE ***STAIRS***.
YOU'RE THE ***GIRL DETECTIVE***! I'M JUST THE ***GIRL COMPUTER WHIZ***! LEAD THE WAY!

THE LOBBY WAS EMPTY. I GUESS THEY TRUSTED THE CAMERAS AND LASER BEAMS TO KEEP OUT THE RIFF RAFF.

NO ADMITTANCE

CREEEEE

WE'D BETTER *HURRY* BEFORE BESS RUNS OUT OF WAYS TO DISTRACT THAT GUARD.

I'M SURE SHE CAN HANDLE HIM, BUT DON'T DAWDLE. THERE MUST BE GUARDS *IN* THE BUILDING, TOO.

HUM
RESO
WHICH MEANS WE'RE *NOT* ALONE.

WE SURE WEREN'T. IT TURNS OUT THAT WALTER REACH, GRUMPY EXECUTIVE, AND NOT MY BIGGEST FAN, HAPPENED TO BE WORKING LATE THAT NIGHT.
HMPH!

HELLO. I'M IN!

ONCE GEORGE HACKED INTO RACKHAM'S EMPLOYEE RECORDS, SHE LOOKED FOR ANYONE WHO STARTED WORKING FOR RACKHAM AROUND THE SAME TIME OUR KLEPTOMANIAC, PAUL BENDER, HIT TOWN.

THEN, WE JUST NEEDED TO SCAN THE PHOTO ID'S TO FIND ONE WHO LOOKED LIKE BENDER.

I BELIEVE WE HAVE A *WINNER!*
HAH!

BING

I CAN'T BELIEVE I DIDN'T FIGURE IT OUT! HE EVEN KEPT THE SAME *INITIALS*.
I GUESS HE'S NOT AS CREATIVE WITH HIS ALIASES AS HE IS WITH HIS *STEALING*. I'LL LOAD HIS FILE ONTO MY LAPTOP AND THEN WE'D BETTER GET GOING!

I SHOULD HAVE SUSPECTED FROM THE START.
BAGEL BOY *PETER BRAVERMAN* WAS NEAR THE CRIME SCENE AND KNEW WAY TOO MUCH!

KLOP KLOP KLOP KLOP
FOOTSTEPS!

THERE WAS NO GETTING OUT THE WAY WE CAME IN.

WHAT THE--?

IN FACT, THERE WAS NO OUT AT ***ALL!***
WE WERE ***TRAPPED!***

SO IT WAS TIME FOR A LITTLE GAME OF HIDE AND SEEK!

I THOUGHT OF JUST LETTING MR. REACH KNOW WHAT WE HAD FOUND, BUT REMEMBERING HOW HE WANTED TO ARREST ME FOR SNOOPING MADE ME THINK THAT WASN'T A GOOD IDEA...

WHAT A WASTE OF ELECTRICITY!
CLIK

IT WASN'T UNTIL HE LEFT THAT I REALIZED I HAD AN EVEN BIGGER PROBLEM.

NANCE? WHERE ARE YOU?
DOWN HERE!

COME ON, LET'S GO! HE MIGHT COME BACK!
I CAN'T! I'M STUCK!

STUCK? HOW'D YOU GET IN? UNGH
OW! I WENT IN BACKWARDS SO I COULD WATCH WHAT WAS GOING ON! NOW I CAN'T GO FORWARD!

SO KEEP GOING BACKWARDS! IT'S GOT TO COME *OUT* SOME- WHERE!
EASIER SAID THAN DONE! THERE'S SOME KIND OF *DROP* BEHIND ME! IT PROBABLY LEADS TO THE *BASEMENT*!

YOU LET GO AND I'LL TRY TO WRIGGLE DOWN. I'LL MEET YOU DOWN- STAIRS!
WAIT! WHAT IF YOU GET STUCK *AGAIN* ALONG THE WAY?

AND EVERYTHING WENT BLACK.

END CHAPTER TWO

# CHAPTER THREE: OUT OF THE VENT, INTO THE FIRE

I DON'T KNOW ***HOW*** LONG I WAS OUT COLD.

I KNEW HE WAS TALKING, BUT I WASN'T EVEN SURE WHAT HE WAS SAYING.

TAKE IT **EASY**! YOU'VE GOT A NASTY **BRUISE**!

VAMOS ROJO

WHOA!

DON'T WORRY, I'VE GOT YOU!

I'M FINE, THANK-YOU, AND I DON'T WANT ANY **BAGELS** JUST NOW... KIND OF YOU TO **ASK**, THOUGH.

POOR GEORGE WAS WAITING FOR ME, EXPECTING ME TO COME OUT AND HEAD BACK TO THE CAR WITH HER.
COME ON, NANCY! WHERE ARE YOU?
ALL SET! I THINK YOUR DISTRIBUTOR CAP JUST CAME LOOSE!
COULD YOU STAY UNDER THE HOOD FOR JUST ANOTHER SECOND OR SO?
I DON'T WANT YOU TO TURN AROUND... I MEAN... I DON'T WANT TO LET YOU GO! I'M HAVING SUCH A NICE TIME!
ME, TOO! WHY DON'T WE HAVE DINNER TOGETHER SOMETIME? CAN YOU GIVE ME YOUR PHONE NUMBER?
YOU KNOW, I'M ALWAYS FORGETTING THAT DARN THING.
THERE'S A SIX IN IT, I JUST KNOW THERE IS...

HEY! I'LL CALL YOU! THANKS FOR THE HELP! GOTTA GO!

SECU
AND YOU, YOU'D BETTER GET RIGHT BACK TO WORK NOW!
GEE, YOU RUN HOT AND COLD, DON'T YOU?!

RUN? I'M NOT RUNNING! THERE'S NOTHING SUSPICIOUS GOING ON HERE! SEE YA!

CALL ME TOMORROW!
LET ME THINK ABOUT IT FOR A WHILE?
SECURTY
NICE WORK MATA HARI!

WEREN'T THERE TWO OF YOU? WHERE'S NANCY?
I WAS HOPING SHE WAS ALREADY OUT HERE!

WELL, SHE'S NOT!
WE WERE SEPARATED. I COULDN'T STAY ANY LONGER WITHOUT GETTING CAUGHT!
WHAT ARE WE GOING TO DO? I CAN'T PRETEND THE CAR'S NOT WORKING AGAIN!

SCREEEEEEECH
WELL, *THAT* CAN'T BE GOOD!

IT'S NOT!
*NANCY* WAS IN THAT CAR!
VROOOM

AND THE DRIVER LOOKS LIKE THE *THIEF* SHE'S BEEN HUNTING!

HANG ON! THIS BABY'S SMALL, BUT SHE'S PACKING MAJOR **HORSE-POWER!**

WHOA!

HEY!
SIT DOWN AND BUCKLE -UP!
SIMMER DOWN! I WANT TO SEE WHAT'S GOING ON!

THIS GUY COULD BE DANGEROUS! SHOULD WE CALL THE POLICE?

WROOOOOOOOOO
I THINK SOMEONE ALREADY DID!

ALL THE EXCITEMENT BROUGHT ME AROUND...
OKAY, PETER, I KNOW YOU STOLE THE CHIP BECAUSE YOU COULDN'T HELP YOURSELF, BUT WHY SEND ME THAT BRACELET?
AWAKE NOW, EH? FEELING BETTER?

I TRY TO CONTROL MYSELF, USUALLY, BUT IT'S SO MUCH FUN!
MOSTLY I STEAL LITTLE STUFF AND NO ONE GETS HURT. BUT WITH ALL THE SECURITY, THAT CHIP WAS SUCH A TEMPTATION!
EVEN SO, WHEN I REALIZED PEOPLE'D GET FIRED, I TRIED TO GIVE IT BACK...

YOU TRIED TO RETURN THE CHIP?
I TOOK IT TO WALTER REACH. I TOLD HIM I WAS JUST TESTING THEIR SECURITY, HOPING HE'D BE IMPRESSED AND NOT FIRE ME.
I REALLY NEED THIS JOB.

"TURNS OUT HE WAS MORE THAN IMPRESSED, HE WAS THRILLED."
SO WE'RE THE ONLY TWO WHO KNOW ABOUT THIS?

IN THAT CASE, I WANT YOU TO HIDE IT!
AND IF YOU TELL ANYONE WHERE IT IS I'LL HAVE YOU FIRED AND ARRESTED! GOT IT?

SO I HAD TO HIDE IT AND KEEP IT SECRET!
I GAVE YOU THAT BRACELET HOPING YOU'D FIND THE CHIP AND JUST RETURN IT, WITHOUT CATCHING ME!
BUT WHY STEAL EVERYTHING ELSE?

THERE WOULD BE TIME ENOUGH FOR QUESTIONS LATER. MORE *IMPORTANT* THINGS WERE COMING UP!
WE'RE BEING **FOLLOWED!**

AND I KNOW EXACTLY WHO IT IS! BESS AND GEORGE!
SO, YOU'D BETTER PULL OVER IF YOU KNOW WHAT'S GOOD FOR YOU!

OH, NO! THE *COPS* ARE RIGHT BEHIND THEM!
I DON'T WANT TO GO BACK TO **PRISON!**

THEN YOU SHOULD DEFINITELY LET ME OUT! STEALING IS ONE THING, KIDNAPPING IS ANOTHER!

KIDNAPPING? I WASN'T KIDNAPPING YOU! I WAS WORRIED SICK ABOUT THAT BUMP ON YOUR HEAD!
I WAS TAKING YOU TO A HOSPITAL!

COPS RIGHT BEHIND ME!
LOOK IN FRONT OF YOU!
HE'S STOPPING!

Y'KNOW, REAL LIFE CAR CHASES JUST AREN'T LIKE THEY ARE IN THE MOVIES OR ON TV.
SKREEEE

WITH THREE CARS GOING REALLY FAST LIKE THAT, IF *ONE* STOPS, ONLY ONE THING CAN HAPPEN!
THUNK

WHICH IS WHY BESS WAS RIGHT TO YELL AT GEORGE. *ALWAYS* WEAR YOUR SAFETY BELT! I KNOW I DO!
WHUNK

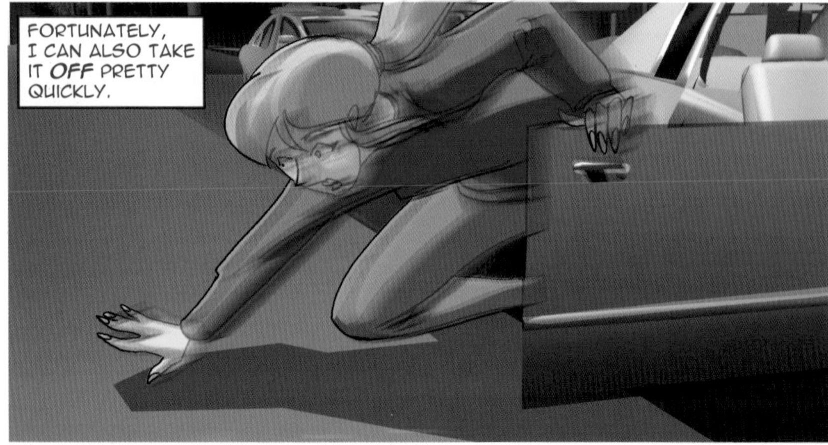
FORTUNATELY, I CAN ALSO TAKE IT OFF PRETTY QUICKLY.

VROOOM

NANCY DREW! I SHOULD HAVE KNOWN.
SEEMS I CAN'T GET A CALL THIS WEEK THAT DOESN'T LEAD ME RIGHT TO YOU AND YOUR FRIENDS.

SORRY TO KEEP YOU BUSY, CHIEF. BUT I THINK WE CAN MAKE IT UP TO YOU...
GEE, NANCE, I CAN PROBABLY FIX THEIR CAR, BUT I'LL NEED TOOLS...

NO, BESS. I KNOW WHO STOLE RACKHAM'S CHIP, REMEMBER?
YEAH. WE EVEN KNOW WHERE HE LIVES.

OKAY THEN, WHY DON'T YOU TAKE ME THERE RIGHT NOW?

THUD

AFTER I CALL FOR ANOTHER CAR.

NOT ONLY DID A NEW CAR COME, BUT IT ALSO DELIVERED A ***SEARCH WARRANT!***

IF I DIDN'T FEEL SORRY FOR PETER BEFORE, I SURE DID WHEN I SAW WHERE HE LIVED.

IT WAS BARELY A SHACK IN THE MIDDLE OF ***NOWHERE!***

HE THOUGHT YOU WERE AFTER **HIM**, CHIEF, SO I'M SURE HE'S LONG GONE.
BAM
BAM
BAM
I'VE GOT THE HIGHWAY PATROL ON THE LOOKOUT FOR HIS CAR, BUT LET'S MAKE **SURE** HE'S NOT HERE.
MR. BRAVER-MAN!

I'LL HAVE TO **BREAK** IT DOWN!
OOMPH!

-CLICK-
I DON'T THINK IT'S **LOCKED,** CHIEF McGINNIS.
ONE... TWO...

THREEEEEEAHHHHH!
CRASH
WHAM

TINKLE
THRUNK

TOO BAD FOR THE HAMILTON INN. YOU BUSTED THEIR BUST!
IT LOOKS LIKE *ALL* THE STOLEN STUFF IS HERE!

BUT I THOUGHT I KNEW A WAY TO GET IT. ESPECIALLY WHEN THE OTHER CROOK WALKED IN.
McGINNIS, I CAME AS SOON AS I GOT THE CALL.
DO YOU... DO YOU HAVE IT?

MR. REACH. I CALLED RACKHAM INDUSTRIES WHEN I THOUGHT WE HAD A LEAD. I'M SORRY, BUT...
IT'S QUITE ALRIGHT REALLY...
WAIT!

I KNOW EXACTLY WHERE THE CHIP IS.
AND I'LL GET IT BACK FOR YOU BY TOMORROW MORNING.
OH... GREAT.

AFTER A QUICK TRIP TO THE EMERGENCY ROOM I HEADED HOME.
I KNEW WALTER REACH WANTED THE CHIP GONE SO HIS DIVISION COULD TAKE OVER, BUT NOW I HAD TO PROVE IT.
REACH KNEW I'D IDENTIFIED PETER AS THE THIEF. AND I TOLD HIM I COULD GET THE CHIP.
BUT HE DIDN'T KNOW PETER HAD TOLD ME ABOUT HIS THREATS.
I COULDN'T BE SURE WHAT HE WOULD DO.
BUT, I KNEW HE WOULD HAVE TO DO SOMETHING.

-RUSTLE-
-RUSTLE-
-RUSTLE-
-GASP!-

A RACCOON, MAYBE?
OR MAYBE NOT.

IT HAD BEEN A LONG NIGHT.
AND IT WASN'T OVER YET.

THE ONLY THING I STILL COULDN'T FIGURE OUT WAS WHY PETER STOLE ALL THOSE OTHER THINGS ON THE BRACELET.

IT JUST DIDN'T MAKE ANY SENSE.
OR MAYBE IT DID, AND I WAS JUST TOO TIRED TO FIGURE IT OUT.

I WAS ASLEEP BEFORE MY HEAD HIT THE PILLOW...
...WHICH IS WHY I WAS TOTALLY UNAWARE WHEN...

...I RECEIVED A *VISITOR*.

AS I SLEPT PEACEFULLY, HE ANXIOUSLY SEARCHED FOR SOMETHING...

...AND *FOUND* IT.

I WOULD'VE SLEPT RIGHT **THROUGH** IT AND HE'D HAVE GOTTEN AWAY IF IT WEREN'T FOR THE FACT THAT...

...I WASN'T **ALONE**!
NO!
HOLD IT RIGHT THERE, MR. REACH!

I'LL TAKE THAT, THANKS.
NANCY SAID YOU WOULD COME FOR THE CHIP!
BUT WHAT IN THE WORLD DO YOU WANT WITH A **CHARM BRACELET**?

I FINALLY FIGURED IT OUT! TAKE A CLOSER LOOK, CHIEF!
THAT CHARM THAT LOOKS LIKE A CHIP-- IS THE MISSING CHIP! I'VE HAD IT ALL ALONG.
PETER BRAVERMAN HAD TO HIDE IT, LIKE REACH ORDERED HIM TO, SO HE HID IT IN PLAIN SIGHT! 
BUT THEN HE STOLE EVERYTHING ELSE JUST SO I WOULDN'T STOP THINKING ABOUT THE BRACELET!

HI, NANCY!
HI, PETER.
LOOKS LIKE YOU DIDN'T GET FAR.

NOPE. I WENT TO FIND LARS JENSEN TO TELL HIM *YOU* HAD THE CHIP.
HE SAID THEY'RE GOING TO TRY AND PUT ME IN SOME SORT OF PROGRAM TO HELP ME WITH MY STEALING PROBLEM.

I TOLD HIM IT WAS ONLY A *PROBLEM* BECAUSE I KEPT GETTING *CAUGHT*, BUT HE DIDN'T LAUGH.
PETER, YOU WOULDN'T KNOW ANYTHING ABOUT A *CAMERA* THAT APPEARED IN NED NICKERSON'S *POCKET*, WOULD YOU?

YEAH, IT WAS *ME!* SORRY! I OVERHEARD HIM SAYING YOU WANTED IT, SO I SLIPPED IT INTO HIS POCKET.
DON'T WORRY, I'LL TELL THE CHIEF.
HEH. I GUESS STEALING *IS* A PROBLEM EVEN IF YOU *DON'T* GET CAUGHT, HUH?

THE CHARGES AGAINST NED WERE DROPPED, BUT I WONDERED IF HE'D BE UPSET THAT I'D SAVED HIM AGAIN.

FOR ME?

TURNED OUT HE WASN'T!

IT'S THE CAMERA! YOU BOUGHT IT FOR ME! THANKS!

PART OF ME JUST WANTED TO SHOW THE STORE-OWNER I COULD! PLUS, I GUESS I FIGURED OUT IT REALLY ISN'T WHO SAVES WHO.

THE IMPORTANT THING IS THAT WE'RE SAFE, RIGHT?

NANCY DREW HERE... IN THE DESERT, OF ALL PLACES. WHICH DESERT, YOU MAY ASK? ALL OF THEM!
IT'S SORT OF A GREATEST HITS OF THE KALAHARI, THE SAHARA, THE GHOBI... WELL, YOU GET THE IDEA!
CHAPTER ONE: CLIMATE CONTROL

I DIDN'T KNOW ***WHAT*** THE PRIZE WAS, BUT ALL I HAD TO HEAR WAS THE WORD ***CLUES*** AND I WAS CHECKING AWAY!

I'D CHECKED THE MEERKATS AND BEARDED DRAGONS...

...CACTI AND SUCCULENTS...

...RATTLESNAKES AND ARMADILLOS.

BUT THE LIST ALSO HAD PERKY ***PENGUINS***, BALMY ***PALM*** TREES AND FEISTY LAND ***CRABS***!

NOT ***DESERT*** ANIMALS YOU SAY? NO PROBLEM...

BECAUSE THE ***ARCTIC*** WAS RIGHT NEXT DOOR!

VERY CONVENIENT FOR A QUICK COOL-OFF AFTER AN HOUR IN THE DESERT!

...ALL WITHOUT EVER SETTING FOOT OUTSIDE THE CITY LIMITS OF RIVER HEIGHTS!
YOU SEE, FAMOUS ENVIRONMENTALIST BILLIONAIRE, CHERI GOALE'S FONDEST DREAM WAS ALWAYS TO BUILD A BIO-DOME ECO-PARK FOR PEOPLE TO LEARN IN AND ENJOY.
AND IN SOME WAYS BILLIONAIRES HAVE AN EASIER TIME MAKING THEIR DREAMS COME TRUE!
AND LUCKY FOR BESS, GEORGE, AND ME, MY DAD, CARSON DREW, IS ONE OF GOALE'S LAWYERS, SO WE WERE GETTING AN EARLY TOUR BY VP JORDAN DENKLE.
MR. DENKLE'S A BIT ON THE ENTHUSIASTIC SIDE. DAD SAYS HE'S DYING TO GET THE PLACE OPEN AND START MAKING MONEY ON THIS INCREDIBLY EXPENSIVE ENDEAVOR.

BUT DAD'S NOT SURE THEY HAVE ENOUGH SAFETY PRECAUTIONS IN PLACE.
I THINK HE MAY BE RIGHT.
THE DOMES ARE MADE OF NATURAL MATERIALS TO AVOID EXPOSING THE ANIMALS TO TOXICITY.
BUT, TO PROTECT YOU FROM THEM, KEEP YOUR DISTANCE AND STAY TOGETHER.
THAT GUY MUST BE THE ANSWER TO THE CLUE, MAMMAL ON THE WHOLE SHELL.
IT'S EITHER AN ARMADILLO... OR A PANGOLIN.
PANGOLIN? YOU MADE THAT UP! IT'S NOT EVEN ON THE LIST! THERE'S NO SUCH THING... EXCEPT MAYBE IN LORD OF THE RINGS!
YEAH? LET'S JUST ASK ONE OF THE SCIENTIFIC ADVISORS!
ONE OF WHOM LOOKED VERY FAMILIAR.

MALACHI CRAVEN!
I WAS AS SURPRISED TO SEE HIM AS HE WAS ME, AND *NEITHER* OF US WAS PLEASED!

BACK IN HILIHILI, HAWAII HE'D DONE SOME VERY *QUESTIONABLE* THINGS TO PROTECT HIS BIO-RESEARCH FACILITY.

HIS LEASE STIPULATED HE COULD ONLY USE THE LAND IN HILIHILI FOR NON-PROFIT RESEARCH, BUT HE WAS SECRETLY FUNDED BY AIKEN BIOTECH TO DEVELOP A NEW SUNSCREEN THAT THEY HOPED WOULD CORNER THE MARKET!
SO... WHAT WAS HE DOING *HERE*?

HIS NAME WASN'T ON OUR LITTLE LIST, BUT THIS WAS ONE CLUE I COULDN'T PASS UP!
UNFORTUNATELY, HE KNEW THE TERRAIN BETTER THAN I DID.

AND, LIKE DAD SAID, THE SAFETY PRECAUTIONS HERE WEREN'T ALL THAT GREAT YET.

I KNEW THE BATS WERE AS AFRAID OF ME AS I WAS OF THEM, BUT THAT DIDN'T HELP EITHER OF US MUCH!

I HATE IT WHEN THEY DO THAT!
BESS WOULD PROBABLY HAVE A FIT IF SHE SAW MY HAIR, BUT THE ONLY THING THAT BOTHERED *ME* ABOUT IT WAS THAT NOW IT MADE IT HARDER TO *SEE*.

MALACHI HAD VANISHED. THAT MEANT THERE WERE PROBABLY SECRET ACCESS *DOORS* IN THIS CREEPY CAVE.

UNFORTUNATELY, DOORS WEREN'T THE *ONLY* THINGS HIDING IN THE DARK.
GASP
AND THE TWO *NEW* EYES GLARING AT ME WERE WAY TOO *BIG* TO BELONG TO A *BAT*!

MR. DENKLE SAID TO KEEP OUR DISTANCE FROM THE ANIMALS AND TO STAY TOGETHER.

OF COURSE, I'D FORGOTTEN TO DO *EITHER*.

I REALLY HOPED HE WAS *EXAGGERATING* WHEN HE SAID *DANGEROUS*.

BUT IF I RECOGNIZED *THIS* BIG GUY...

...DANGEROUS WAS AN UNDERSTATEMENT.

YEEEIII!

MY LIST WAS GONE, BUT I DIDN'T NEED IT TO CLUE IN ON A KOMODO DRAGON!

THEY GROW AS LONG AS TEN FEET, HUNT IN PACKS AND EAT ***HORSES!***
NICE HORSE-EATING LIZARD! GO AWAY NOW! PLEASE?

THEIR SALIVA ISN'T VENOMOUS, BUT IT'S SO FULL OF BACTERIA AND OTHER FILTH, IT'S JUST AS BAD.

EVEN A SMALL BITE CAN BE ***DEADLY!***
***HEEELLLLLP!***

THOUGH MOST OF THE BIO-DOME WAS NATURAL, THESE CAVE WALLS WEREN'T! AND I GUESS THEY WEREN'T BUILT TO HOLD THE COMBINED WEIGHT OF A KOMODO AND A GIRL DETECTIVE.
LUCKY ME!
BESS AND GEORGE DIDN'T KNOW WHAT TO DO WHEN THE KOMODO CAME CHARGING OUT OF THE CAVE...
I SUPPOSE YOU'RE GOING TO TELL ME THAT'S A PANGOLIN, TOO!
NOPE! JUST GONNA SCREAM!
YAAAAAAHHHH!
LOOK OUT! JUST STAND BACK AND LET IT GO!
DUH!
LIKE WE WERE GOING TO PET IT!

YOU KNOW, IT'S FUNNY, BUT THAT BEAST SEEMED--
DON'T YOU DARE SAY MORE AFRAID THAN WE WERE.
I DON'T KNOW IF DRAGONS GET SCARED, BUT IT SURE SEEMED SPOOKED.
THOUGHT YOU'D GO OFF ON YOUR OWN TO FIND THE REALLY EXOTIC ANIMALS, EH?!
ACTUALLY IT FOUND ME. AND I'M GUESSING IT'S NOT CHECKING ME OFF ITS LIST.
THAT WAS A KOMODO DRAGON! WHAT WERE YOU DOING TO INCUR THE WRATH OF A KOMODO DRAGON?
DRAGON?! THAT'S NOT ON OUR DESERT LIST, GEORGE!
NO, IT WOULDN'T BE. IT'S AN ISLAND CREATURE.
IT MUST HAVE GOTTEN IN THE SAME WAY MALACHI CRAVEN GOT OUT. BUT IF THERE'S A HIDDEN DOOR IN HERE, I CAN'T FIND IT.

I FILLED THEM IN ON MY LAST ENCOUNTER WITH CRAVEN.
WELL, IF HE'S RUNNING FROM YOU, I'M GUESSING HE'S NOT A GOOD GUY.
MAYBE. HE MAY JUST HAVE SOME BAD MEMORIES OF ME.
**HERE** YOU ARE! WE'VE GOT TO MOVE ON. APPARENTLY SOME ANIMAL FROM ONE OF THE OTHER DOMES WOUND UP IN HERE, AND IT'S PRETTY **DANGEROUS**.

YEAH! I UH... GUESS WE SHOULD GET GOING THEN!

THE ISLAND DOME SHOULD BE GREAT! C'MON!
THIS TIME LET'S DO WHAT THE MAN SAID, STICK TOGETHER AND KEEP **AWAY** FROM THE ANIMALS!

BACK OUT IN THE RIVER HEIGHTS AIR, IT WAS A SHORT WALK FROM THE DESERT TO THE ISLANDS.
MR. DENKLE! IF A KOMODO DRAGON CAN ESCAPE FROM ONE ENVIRO-DOME INTO ANOTHER-- WHAT'S TO STOP IT FROM ESCAPING TO RIVER HEIGHTS?!
ER...
Bustard
AND WHY WOULD A KOMODO DRAGON *WANT* TO LEAVE THE COMFORT OF ITS *NATIVE* HABITAT FOR ONE *LESS SUITABLE*?!
UM...
OH.

THIS PLACE WAS *FINE* YESTERDAY! WHAT IS IT?!
NOT EXACTLY AN ISLAND PARADISE, HUH?
IT LOOKS LIKE SOME KIND OF *FUNGUS*.

I GUESS THEY HADN'T WORKED OUT ALL THE KINKS IN THE SYSTEM YET!

I REALIZED THIS PROBABLY WASN'T A GOOD TIME TO POINT THAT OUT TO MR. DENKLE, BUT WHEN THERE'S A MYSTERY, I JUST CAN'T HELP MYSELF.
MR. DENKLE, YOU SAID THE ECO-SYSTEMS WERE CREATED USING ALL NATURAL MATERIALS.
COULD THIS FUNGUS BE SOMETHING YOU CREATED -- BY *ACCIDENT*?

I DON'T KNOW.
*MALACHI CRAVEN* IS OUR HEAD OF BIO-DEVELOPMENT. HE'D BETTER BE ABLE TO *EXPLAIN* THIS DISASTER IF HE WANTS TO KEEP HIS JOB.

HE WAS IN THE DESERT DOME, BUT HE DISAPPEARED IN A CAVE.
YES, PASSAGEWAYS CONNECT ALL THE ENVIRONMENTS TO THE CONTROL CENTER. I'LL HAVE HIM BACK HERE IN A MOMENT.

BACK ON HILIHILI, CRAVEN EXPERIMENTED WITH LOCAL VEGETATION AND WORRIED HE'D TIPPED THE DELICATE BALANCE OF NATURE.
I COULDN'T HELP WONDERING IF HE WAS AT IT *AGAIN*.
WHATEVER IT WAS SEEMED TO BE CORRODING EVERY *PLANT* AND *TREE* IT TOUCHED-- *FAST*.

HMM. THE DRAGON WAS SPOOKED, BUT HE DIDN'T LOOK UNHEALTHY. AND THIS SEA TURTLE LOOKS *FINE*.
SO DOES THIS PRETTY PARROT!
*SQUAWWK* OUR GOALS ARE YOUR GOALS!

THEY TAUGHT HIM TO *GREET* GOALE GUESTS!
"A COLORFUL CONVERSATIONALIST"-- *CHECK*!

WE NEED TO SEAL THIS DOME UNTIL WE FIND OUT WHAT'S HAPPENED. MEANWHILE, I'M AFRAID YOU'LL HAVE TO LEAVE.
BUT, THE FUNGUS SEEMS HARMLESS TO US AND THE OTHER ANIMALS! SO IT'S STILL A MYSTERY WHAT SCARED THE KOMODO DRAGON.

THE FUNGUS ITSELF MAY NOT BE HARMFUL TO ANIMAL LIFE, BUT IF IT IS DECOMPOSING THE PLANTS, IT MIGHT CORRODE THE WOODEN DOME FRAME.
THE WHOLE STRUCTURE COULD COLLAPSE!

DARN. I WAS HOPING TO SEE SOME OF THE MORE EXOTIC CREATURES ON THE LIST.
GULP! TRY TURNING AROUND...
TURNS OUT FLORA AND FAUNA WEREN'T THE ONLY ISLAND LIFE IN THE DOME!

APPARENTLY THERE WAS A CREATURE FROM AN ISLAND MYTH HERE, TOO! AND I HAPPENED TO KNOW HIS NAME WAS...
OKALA KANE!
THAT'S NOT ON THE LIST!

OKALA KANE IS PART OF A HILIHILI LEGEND.
THE GODDESS PELE CREATED HIM TO ENACT VENGEANCE, GIVING HIM THE POWER TO UNLEASH NATURAL DISASTERS.
THESE DOMES ARE AN AFFRONT AGAINST THE GODS! THE PESTILENCE IS THEIR WAY OF PUNISHING YOU!
CATCH THAT-- WHATEVER IT IS-- NOW!
H-HOLD IT RIGHT THERE!
ALL THIS MUST BE DESTROYED!
AND THAT AGAIN POINTED TO MALACHI CRAVEN!

MR. DENKLE KEPT ORDERING THAT POOR GUARD INTO THE WATERFALL A DOZEN TIMES, BUT THE RESULT WAS ALWAYS THE SAME.
NOTHING! IT'S EMPTY! HE DIS-APPEARED.
IS THERE A SECRET PASSAGE THROUGH THERE?
NONE I KNOW OF.
YOU'LL WANT TO CALL THE POLICE AND EVEN THE CENTER FOR DISEASE CONTROL.
THE PUBLICITY WILL RUIN US!
I CAN'T RISK THE PRESS GETTING HOLD OF THIS STORY!
WE HAVE TO OPEN NEXT WEEK AND START RECOUPING THE BILLIONS IT COST THE GOALE COMPANY TO BUILD.
I CAN HELP.

YOU? THAT'S RIGHT, YOU'RE THE LOCAL GIRL DETECTIVE I'VE READ ABOUT, AREN'T YOU?
I'VE HELPED OUT NOW AND THEN.
AND SOLVING THIS MYSTERY IS REALLY JUST A CONTINUATION OF THE SCAVENGER HUNT.
I'M NOT SURE HOW YOU COULD STOP NANCY FROM TRYING TO FIGURE THIS OUT.
WELL... I SUPPOSE, IF YOU REALLY THINK YOU CAN HELP...
HERE'S AN EMPLOYEE MAP OF THE PARK THAT INCLUDES THE SECRET PASSAGEWAYS. IF YOU SEE ANYTHING STRANGE, CALL SECURITY IMMEDIATELY.
AREA MAP
OKAY, BOSS, WHERE DO WE START?
YOU GUYS CHECK FOR OTHER FLORA AND FAUNA NOT IN THE RIGHT DOME.

ME, I WENT OFF TO TRACK DOWN AN OLD ACQUAINTANCE.
CONTROL ROOM

MALACHI CRAVEN!
YOU! HOW DID YOU KNOW I WAS IN HERE?
ACTUALLY, MR. DENKLE *TOLD* ME WHERE HE'D BE, BUT I SAW NO REASON TO TELL CRAVEN THAT.

AND HOW DO YOU ALWAYS MANAGE TO BE AROUND WHEN THERE'S SOME MYSTERIOUS *DISASTER*?!
ME? YOU'RE PRETTY GOOD AT THAT YOURSELF! AND WHY DOES THE NAME *OKALA KANE* SEEM TO FOLLOW YOU AROUND?

OKALA KANE! WHAT DO YOU MEAN?
YOU DON'T KNOW? HE ACTUALLY SHOWED UP IN THE ISLAND DOME.
MALACHI SEEMED AS SHOCKED ABOUT OKALA KANE'S PRESENCE AS I'D BEEN. IN FACT, HE INSISTED ON TAKING ME BACK TO THE ISLAND DOME TO TELL HIM EVERYTHING.
THIS WAS NOT HOW A GUILTY MAN WOULD ACT, SO I WAS STARTING TO WONDER...
SHOW ME EXACTLY WHERE YOU SAW HIM ESCAPE.
CRAAAACK
THROUGH THERE.
THERE'S NOT SUPPOSED TO BE ANY PASSAGES THOUGH THERE, BUT THERE MUST BE!
BUT YOU KNOW, YOUR COLLEAGUE SAID THE FUNGUS MIGHT EAT AWAY AT THE STRUCTURE.

I DON'T FEEL ANY OPENING OR LATCH.
MR. CRAVEN? I KNOW I CAN GET WRAPPED UP IN A MYSTERY, BUT DO YOU THINK MAYBE WE SHOULD FIND *ANOTHER* EXIT, AND *FAST*?!
CRAAAAKKKK
BUT IT WAS DEFINITELY *TOO LATE* FOR THAT!

HE WAS RIGHT! WE STOOD IN THE TINY SPACE AS A WALL OF DEBRIS RAINED DOWN IN FRONT OF US.

WE WERE ***TRAPPED!***

END CHAPTER ONE

CHAPTER TWO:
ECO-TERROR
TAP
WHIRRR
JUST WHEN I WAS SURE WE'D BE
*CRUSHED* LIKE PALMETTO BUGS...

WE STUMBLED ON THE SECRET *EXIT!*

GET AWAY
FROM THERE!
THE DOME'S
COMING
DOWN!
I WAS GLAD SOMEONE
*ELSE* HAD NOTICED.

AND LOTS OF IT!

NANCE, YOU ALL RIGHT?!
MALACHI, I HOLD YOU PERSONALLY RESPONSIBLE FOR THIS!

YOU THINK I HAD SOMETHING TO DO WITH THIS?!
WHO ELSE?!

ARE YOU OR ARE YOU NOT IN CHARGE OF BALANCING THE ECOSYSTEM'S ECO-THING, OR WHATEVER YOU CALL IT!
YES. YES, I'M IN CHARGE.

AND THE TROPICAL STUFF IS SUPPOSED TO BE YOUR FORTE! IRONIC YOU'D SCREW UP THAT PARTICULAR DOME!
OBVIOUSLY CHERI MADE A BIG MISTAKE TAKING A CHANCE ON YOU!

THIS CAN'T HAVE BEEN AN ACCIDENT! THIS KIND OF FUNGUS DOESN'T JUST APPEAR OUT OF NOWHERE IN A HEALTHY ENVIRONMENT!
THEN WHAT DO YOU SUGGEST HAPPENED, MR. SCIENCE?!

SABOTAGE!
RIDICULOUS! CHERI HASN'T AN ENEMY IN THE WORLD! WHO WOULD WANT TO HURT THIS PROJECT?

SO SAVE YOUR THEORIES FOR THE TABLOIDS! ONCE YOU ASSESS THE DAMAGE HERE, WE'LL ASSESS YOUR FUTURE WITH GOALE!

DENKLE WAS PRETTY HARD ON MALACHI.
I GUESS FOLKS GET TESTY WHEN WHOLE WORLDS ARE DESTROYED.
I KIND OF UNDER-STAND HIS REACTION...

...MALACHI'S HISTORY OF SECRET EXPERIMENTS WOULD MAKE ANYONE SUSPICIOUS!

YOU **MUST** GET THAT ANTI-FUNGAL AGENT HERE ***IMMEDIATELY***!
FROM THE WAY HE WAS ACTING, I SUSPECTED SOME-THING ABOUT MALACHI, TOO.

...THAT HE WAS ***INNOCENT***!

YOU ***REALLY*** THINK THIS WAS SABOTAGE?!
WHAT ELSE?!

THEN LET US HELP!
YOU?! HELP ME?

YOUR HELP IN HILIHILI WAS RESPONSIBLE FOR SHUTTING DOWN MY ENTIRE RESEARCH FACILITY!
DO YOU KNOW HOW HARD IT WAS FOR ME TO GET A JOB AFTER THAT? ANY JOB?

JUST STAY AWAY FROM ME! FAR AWAY!
TALK ABOUT UN-GRATEFUL!
NOT REALLY. DENKLE HAS REASONS FOR NOT TRUSTING MALACHI. MALACHI HAS REASONS FOR NOT TRUSTING ME.
OF COURSE HE WAS DOING ILLEGAL RESEARCH ON THE ISLAND. BUT HE CERTAINLY SEEMED CHANGED.

IT MUST HAVE BEEN HARD FOR DENKLE TO CALL CHERI GOALE. BUT THE PARK'S CREATOR AND FOUNDATION HEAD WAS THERE IN MINUTES, DRIVEN BY HER SON, DWAYNE.
I WAS IMPRESSED TO SEE THAT DESPITE ALL HER MONEY, SHE DROVE A LITTLE HYBRID, ALMOST LIKE MINE!

CHERI, THIS IS MY DAUGHTER, NANCY.
YOUR FATHER'S TOLD ME SO MUCH ABOUT YOU, NANCY!
HER ENTIRE LIFE WAS DEVOTED TO ENVIRONMENTALISM...

...AND THIS ECO-PARK HAD BEEN HER LIFELONG DREAM...
IT'S GOOD TO FINALLY MEET THE FAMOUS GIRL DETECTIVE.
I'M SORRY WE HAVE TO MEET UNDER SUCH, WELL, DISASTROUS CIRCUMSTANCES.

I'M JUST GLAD NO ONE WAS *HARMED*.

...BUT SHE SEEMED *STRANGELY* UNRUFFLED.

I THINK ALL THE ANIMALS MADE IT OUT SAFELY, TOO. BUT, IT SURE RATTLED SOME NERVES, EH, LITTLE FELLA?!

EEEP!

I'M SAYING MAYBE WE SHOULD JUST *SCRAP* OUR PLANS AND SHUT THE PLACE DOWN.

SHUT IT DOWN?!

SO, MALACHI, THE *FIRST* PERSON I'D SUSPECT, WAS ACTING TOTALLY INNOCENT, WHILE CHERI GOALE, THE *LAST* PERSON I'D SUSPECT, WAS ACTING KIND OF *SUSPICIOUS*!

AND MAYBE YOU SHOULD MAKE YOURSELF USEFUL, DWAYNE, AND HELP OUR GUESTS WITH THEIR QUIZZES WHILE THE GROWN-UPS TALK BUSINESS!
CHERI, DO YOU REALIZE WHAT WOULD BE INVOLVED...
I COULD USE HELP WITH THESE CLUES-
YEAH, LIKE WHAT CLUES INDICATE THE DOME IS ABOUT TO FALL ON YOU!
EXCUSE MY COUSIN'S SENSE OF HUMOR! I HAVE SOME LEGIT QUESTIONS ABOUT THE QUIZ, AND I'M SURE YOU KNOW ALL THE ANSWERS.
HE'S RICH. HE'S CUTE. HE'S AVAILABLE...
HE'S BESS'S.

BUT, FUNNY THING ABOUT WILD ANIMALS, THEY *RUN* WHEN YOU CHASE THEM-- EVEN IF YOU'RE TRYING TO SAVE THEM.

BUT THERE'S MORE THAN ONE WAY TO DO DETECTIVE WORK. AND... OH, DARN! HERE, I'D ONCE AGAIN FOUND MYSELF INADVERTENTLY *EAVESDROPPING.*

IT'D BE RUDE TO INTERRUPT BY MAKING MY PRESENCE KNOWN. AND MORE USEFUL IF I *DIDN'T*.

YOU KNOW WE CAN'T SHUT DOWN! WHAT ARE YOU THINKING?
THIS DOME COLLAPSE IS A TOTAL DISASTER. WE'LL HAVE TO AT LEAST DELAY THE OPENING!

THERE WAS ANOTHER ADVANTAGE, TOO. I WAS BEING SO STILL, MY LITTLE FRIEND THOUGHT IT WAS SAFE TO COME OUT.

AND I WOULD HAVE CAUGHT HIM, IF DENKLE HADN'T BELLOWED!
DELAY?!
ALL THE PRESS IS OUT! TALK ABOUT A DISASTER! EVEN A DELAY WOULD COST MILLIONS!

YOU HAVE STOCKHOLDERS TO THINK OF, NOT TO MENTION YOUR PRECIOUS FOUNDATIONS.
WHERE WOULD ALL THOSE ANIMALS BE IF THE FUNDING FOR THEIR PRESERVATION RAN OUT?
I REALIZE IT WOULD BE DIFFICULT TO REPAIR THE MONETARY DAMAGE. BUT, REALLY, WHAT ABOUT THE FUNGUS?!
HOW CAN WE POSSIBLY KNOW THAT IT WOULD BE SAFE TO OPEN ON THURSDAY?
WHAT HAPPENS IF ANOTHER DOME COLLAPSES, WITH MORE PEOPLE IN IT?
AS YOUR ATTORNEY, I'D RECOMMEND BEFORE YOU CONTACT ANYONE ABOUT DELAYING THE OPENING, WAIT AND SEE IF THE ANTI-FUNGAL MALACHI IS GETTING CAN CONTAIN THIS.
AT LAST, SOMEONE MAKES SENSE! THANK YOU, CARSON.

DR. MALACHI IS VERY COMMITTED TO THIS PROJECT. WHATEVER HIS HISTORY, I DON'T THINK HE'S RESPONSIBLE FOR ***THIS***.

IT WOULD SURE BE ***EMBARRASSING*** IF HE IS, CONSIDERING HOW THE BOARD TRIED TO TALK YOU ***OUT*** OF HIRING HIM.

*GOTCHA!*

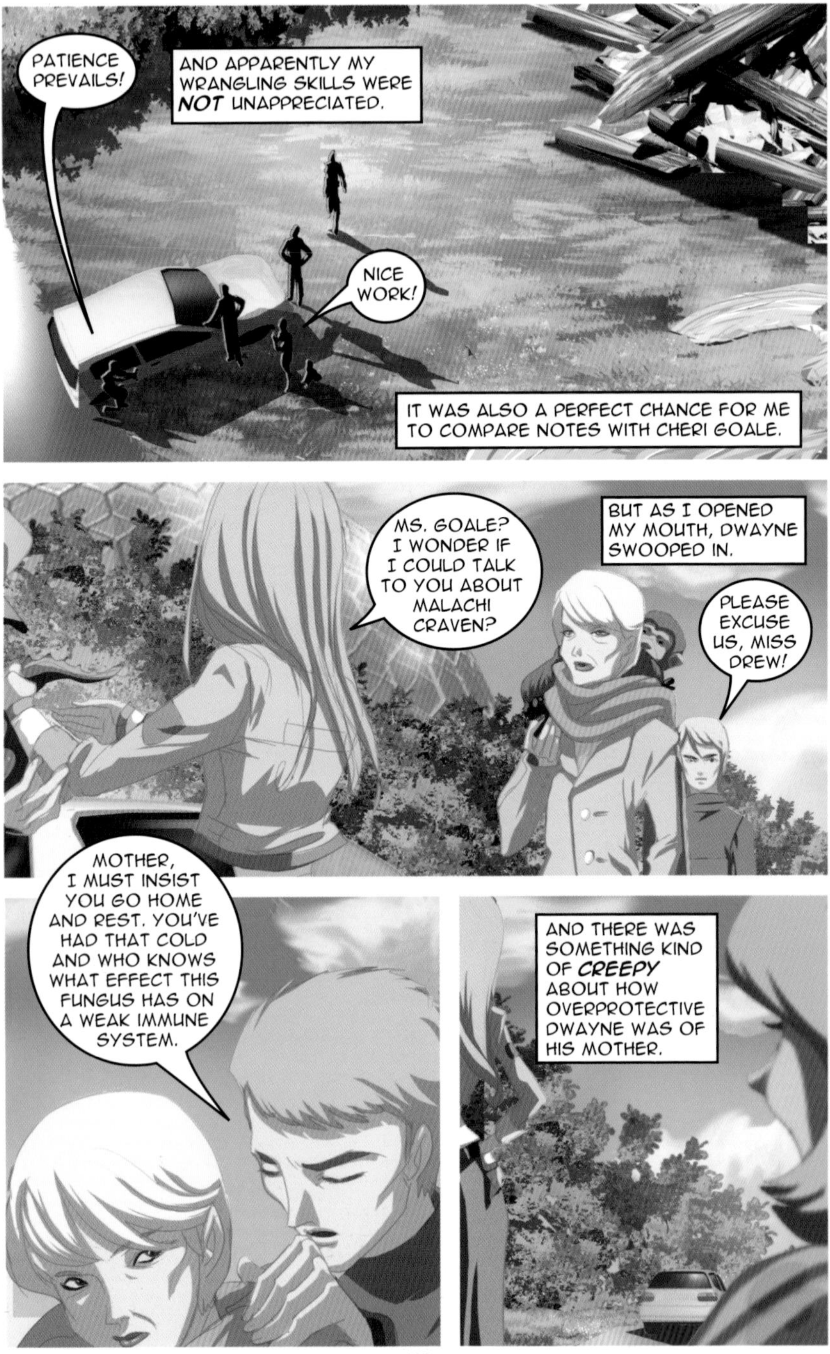

MS. GOALE? I WONDER IF I COULD TALK TO YOU ABOUT MALACHI CRAVEN?

BUT AS I OPENED MY MOUTH, DWAYNE SWOOPED IN.

PLEASE EXCUSE US, MISS DREW!

MOTHER, I MUST INSIST YOU GO HOME AND REST. YOU'VE HAD THAT COLD AND WHO KNOWS WHAT EFFECT THIS FUNGUS HAS ON A WEAK IMMUNE SYSTEM.

AND THERE WAS SOMETHING KIND OF ***CREEPY*** ABOUT HOW OVERPROTECTIVE DWAYNE WAS OF HIS MOTHER.

I THINK GEORGE WAS RIGHT. IN FACT, HE WAS IN SUCH A ***HURRY*** TO GET HIS MOM HOME, HE NEARLY ***HIT*** THE FUNGICIDE TRUCK COMING IN!

I'VE GOT A HUNCH THERE'S SOMETHING ABOUT THE GOALES THAT WARRANTS INVESTIGATING.

AND I HAVE A HUNCH ABOUT WHO'LL ***DO*** THE INVESTIGATING!

BESS WAS RIGHT, OF COURSE. I SPENT THE ENTIRE *NIGHT* THINKING ABOUT THE CASE. I WOULD HAVE EVEN FORGOTTEN TO BRUSH MY TEETH IF HANNAH, OUR HOUSEKEEPER, HADN'T REMINDED ME.
BUT ONE THING I DECIDED WAS THAT IF THE DOME'S COLLAPSE WAS THE WORK OF A SABOTEUR, WE WERE GOING TO *FIND* HIM...
...WHETHER MALACHI CRAVEN LIKED IT OR NOT.

AND EXPLORING ONE OF THE DOMES THAT WAS STILL STANDING, SEEMED LIKE A GOOD PLACE TO START.
THE HILLS ARE ALIVE WITH THE SOUND OF--
--BESS TRYING TO MAKE MUUUSIC!
I CAN'T HELP IT IF I SPEND MORE MONEY ON CLOTHES THAN ON SINGING LESSONS.
SO THAT'S WHY YOU SHOULD BE SEEN AND NOT HEARD.
I RESENT THAT!

THAT MUST BE ONE OF THE EMPLOYEE PASSAGEWAYS. IT'S BEEN LEFT OPEN.

ONE OF THE WORKERS MAY BE AROUND. ARE YOU SURE DENKLE SAID IT WAS OKAY FOR US TO BE IN HERE?

MAYBE THEY WERE UP HERE FIXING ***THAT***.

THAT'S WEIRD.

THEY ***CONTROL*** THE WIND, SO THEY WOULDN'T LET IT GET STRONG ENOUGH TO UPROOT TREES.

AND I DON'T THINK HE'S THE WARM FUZZY KIND OF SASQUATCH YOU SEE ON BELIEVE IT OR NOT!

REALLY? I WAS JUST THINKING...

RUN!

RUMBLE RUMBLE
RUMBLE
GOOD THINKING!

RUMBLE
RUMBLE
RUMBLE
RUMBLE
LUCKILY, BOULDERS MOVE SLOWLY ENOUGH TO BE EASILY DODGED.

UNLUCKILY, IT LOOKED LIKE WE WEREN'T THE TARGET AFTER ALL, AND BOULDERS BUILD UP MOMENTUM AS THEY ROLL DOWNHILL...
RUMBLE
RUMBLE
RUMBLE

SO I GUESS THE MORAL IS THAT SASQUATCHES WHO LIVE IN GLASS DOMES SHOULDN'T ROLL BOULDERS!

WHAT THE DEVIL-- ?

WHAT ON EARTH HAPPENED HERE?!
SASQUACH, EH?! LOOKS LIKE MALACHI CRAVEN, TO ME!
I KNOW IT SOUNDS WACKY, MR. DENKLE, BUT A SASQUATCH PUSHED IT FROM UP THERE!
NO!

WE'VE GOT HIM RED-HANDED! I'M CALLING THE POLICE AND HAVING THAT WALKING DISASTER ***ARRESTED!***

RIGHT! I'LL JUST TELL CHIEF McGINNIS TO PUT OUT AN APB FOR SASQUATCH, PROTECTOR OF THE WOOD!

BUT, IT WAS A SASQUATCH!

OKAY, SO IT'S SOMEONE IN A SASQUATCH ***COSTUME!***

HOW COULD HE HAVE CHANGED OUT OF HIS ***COSTUME*** IN ONE MINUTE?!

THERE WAS NO REASONING WITH DENKLE; HE PLANNED ON PRESSING CHARGES! MINUTES LATER, CHIEF McGINNIS WAS THERE TO TAKE CRAVEN IN.

BUT NOT BEFORE HE SLIPPED ME A PIECE OF PAPER.

LOOKS LIKE I'LL HAVE TO TRUST YOU.

TAKE THESE ACCESS CODES FOR THE REMAINING DOME. YOU MAY BE OUR ONLY HOPE FOR FINDING THE ***REAL*** SABOTEUR!

DOES THAT SAY WHAT I ***THINK*** IT SAYS?

YEAH.

LOOKS LIKE WE'LL HAVE TO PUT ON SOME ***WARMER*** CLOTHES.

ARCTIC ZONE

021098

WELL, IF WE DON'T SOLVE THE MYSTERY, AT LEAST THIS'LL GET US CLOSER TO FINDING THE REST OF THE ANSWERS TO THAT DARN QUIZ!

HURRY UP! I'M SWEATING TO DEATH!
IT SURE TOOK THAT GUARD LONG ENOUGH TO GO ON BREAK. IT MUST BE CLOSE TO MIDNIGHT.
ONCE WE'RE INSIDE WE SHOULDN'T BE NOTICED.

YEAH, WHO'D BE CRAZY ENOUGH TO LOOK AROUND IN HERE?!
OTHER THAN US, YOU MEAN?

THE GOOD NEWS IS THAT ANYTHING IN HERE HASN'T GOT A LOT OF PLACES TO HIDE...
UH, AGAIN, SOMEONE WOULD BE US! I MEAN, WE MIGHT WANT TO HIDE, TOO, RIGHT?

TRACKS! BIG ONES!

HMM. NOTHING ABOUT GIANT HUMAN-LIKE TRACKS ON THE LIST OF CLUES.
M-M-MAYBE BECAUSE IT ISN'T ON THE LIST!

THIS TIME ONLY TWO OF US KNEW THE NAME.
AROOOOOOOOOH!
YETI!
A-A-A WHAT YOU SAID!

NANCY, GET THAT DOOR OPEN, QUICK!
I CAN'T. THE CODE ISN'T *WORKING*!
AND THERE'S NO PLACE TO HIDE!
SO WE'RE TRAPPED...
...WITH *HIM*!
END CHAPTER TWO

HE, IT, CAME AT US FAST AND ANGRY!
I KNEW GEORGE COULD BE BRAVE BUT I WAS SURPRISED TO SEE HER ACTUALLY GRABBING AT IT!
YEEEIII!
CHAPTER THREE:
THERE IS NO BETTER YETI
AS FOR ME, NORMALLY, I'M A PEACEFUL KIND OF GIRL DETECTIVE, BUT GIVEN THAT WE HAD NO PLACE TO RUN...

FIGHTING SEEMED NOT ONLY LIKE A GOOD IDEA, IT SEEMED LIKE THE ONLY IDEA!
BACK OFF, FUR-FACE!
BAD YETI! BAD!
I TRIED TO GIVE IT A LITTLE WARNING BOP ON THE HEAD.
BUT I MAY HAVE GOTTEN CARRIED AWAY.

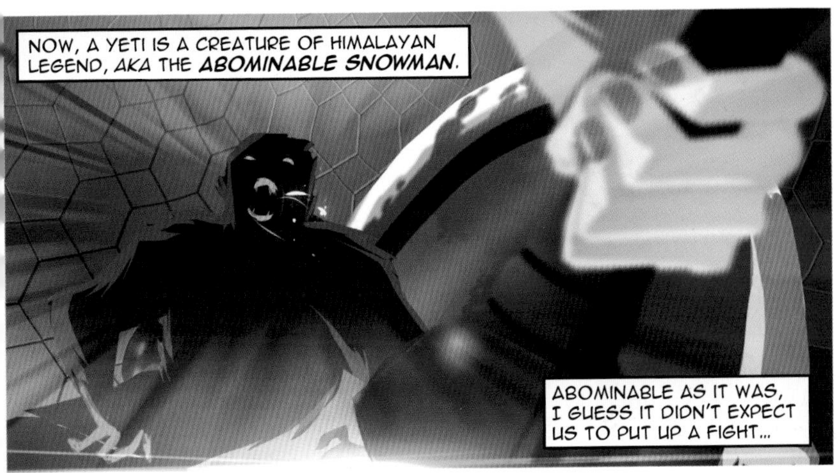
NOW, A YETI IS A CREATURE OF HIMALAYAN LEGEND, AKA THE ABOMINABLE SNOWMAN.
ABOMINABLE AS IT WAS, I GUESS IT DIDN'T EXPECT US TO PUT UP A FIGHT...

RRRREIIII!
THE POOR THING SEEMED SO CONFUSED, I ALMOST FELT BAD FOR HIM WHEN HE BACKED INTO THE KEYPAD, SOMEHOW THE SPARKS SET HIS FUR ON FIRE.

BUT WHEN IT CHARGED AT ME, I WENT BACK TO FEELING BAD FOR ME!

FORTUNATELY, IT WAS JUST TRYING TO GET *AWAY*... PROBABLY TO EXTINGUISH ITS SMOLDERING FUR.

IT'S HURT! I'M GOING AFTER IT.

SHOULD WE COME WITH YOU?!
NO! SEE IF YOU CAN GET THAT KEYPAD TO STOP *SIZZLING*.

IF WE TRY TO COOL IT OFF WITH SNOW IT COULD SHORT OUT MORE WIRES.
AND THAT WOULD BE BAD!

WORSE, EVEN.
THIS THING LOOKS LIKE IT'S PART OF THE CLIMATE CONTROL SYSTEM. IF IT MELTS, IT COULD WHACK THE WHOLE SYSTEM!

UH, BESS, THAT PANEL ISN'T ALL THAT'S MELTING!

THE REFRIGERATION WASN'T JUST OFF, IT SEEMED SOME-ONE HAD TURNED UP THE HEAT.

THE ARCTIC WORLD WAS LIKE AN ICE CREAM STORE INSIDE A MICROWAVE...
..AND *ANIMALS* DO *NOT* BELONG IN MICROWAVES!

I DECIDED THE YETI WAS BIG ENOUGH TO FEND FOR ITSELF.

RIGHT NOW, WE HAD TO GET THE MORE HELPLESS, AND LESS MYTHICAL, CREATURES, TO SAFETY BEFORE THEY WERE WASHED AWAY!

BUT, WHERE ***WAS*** SAFETY?!

...UNTIL OUR MYTHICAL PAL SHOWED US THE WAY!

LOOK, A PASSAGEWAY!

YEEEOOIII!

HURRY!
WE CAN HERD AS MANY ANIMALS AS POSSIBLE TO THAT PASSAGE-WAY.

THE PASSAGEWAY LED DIRECTLY TO THE PARK'S ANIMAL INFIRMARY!

MEANING OUR FRIEND NOT ONLY KNEW THE PARK WELL, BUT WAS ALSO WORRIED ABOUT THE ANIMALS, MAKING HIM AN ABOMINABLE-BUT-SOMETIMES-HELPFUL SNOWMAN.

BESS AND GEORGE WERE GLAD TO CLUE IN ON MORE ANIMALS.
NOW THEY EACH NEEDED ONLY ONE MORE TO COMPLETE THE QUIZ.

GRRR-ATCH

EEEEK!
SOME THANKS FOR SAVING YOUR MANGY BUTT.
BUT, THEY WERE NOT SO JOLLY ABOUT HAVING TO CORRAL A PACK OF CONFUSED WOLVES!

WE SOMEHOW MANAGED TO GET **ALL** THE ANIMALS OUT OF THE FLOODING DOME AND INTO THE INFIRMARY...

...AT LEAST **ALL** THOSE WE COULD **FIND**.

HAVING THEM **ALL TOGETHER** SHOULD MAKE IT EASY TO FIND THE ANSWER TO THIS LAST CLUE...

MIGRATORY ANIMAL WHO IS THE ONLY NATURAL ENEMY OF THE POLAR BEAR.

WOW! WHAT WOULD BE A **POLAR BEAR'S** ENEMY!

I'M NOT SURE THESE ANIMALS **SHOULD BE** ALL TOGETHER. MAYBE WE'D BETTER **CALL** SOMEONE TO GET OVER HERE WITH SOME LEASHES?!

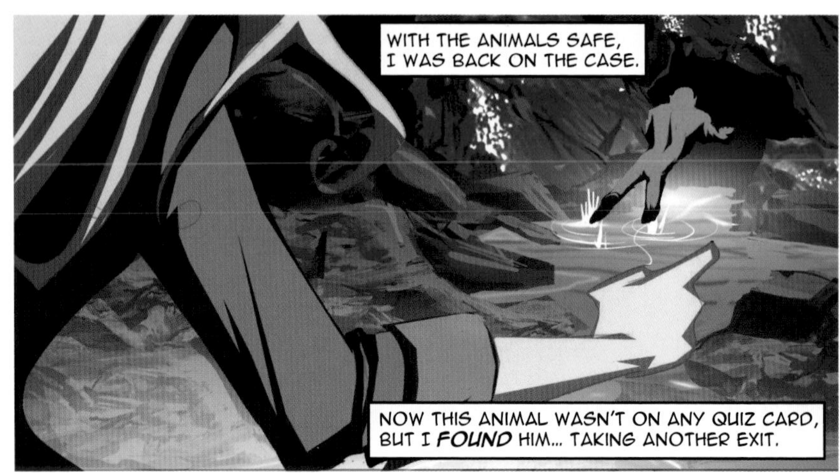
WITH THE ANIMALS SAFE, I WAS BACK ON THE CASE.
NOW THIS ANIMAL WASN'T ON ANY QUIZ CARD, BUT I *FOUND* HIM... TAKING ANOTHER EXIT.

HE'D *SEEN* ME.
SEEMS HE DIDN'T WANT TO CHAT ABOUT OUR TEAM EFFORT ON THE RECENT DISASTER.

HE WAS TOO BUSY *RUNNING* WITH THOSE *BIG FEET* OF HIS.
*STOP!* I JUST WANT TO ASK--

...BUT I'D SWEAR HE WAS ***AVOIDING*** ME.

THE RIVER'S CURRENT WAS REALLY ***STRONG***, WHICH HAD ME THINKING JUST FOR A SECOND THAT MAYBE THIS ***WASN'T*** JUST SOME GUY IN A COSTUME.

AND IF ***THAT*** WAS TRUE, I WANTED TO KNOW MORE ABOUT THIS CREATURE, HOW IT STAYED HIDDEN FOR SO LONG, WHAT MADE IT SUCH A STRONG SWIMMER-- DID IT HAVE ***HOLLOW HAIR*** LIKE A POLAR BEAR?

NOT THAT I THOUGHT THE INFORMATION WAS WORTH *DROWNING* FOR.

HMM. WET YETI WAS MUCH *SLIMMER* THAN DRY YETI.
IF ITS *SIZE* WAS DECEPTIVE, MAYBE SO WAS ITS *STRENGTH*.

ALL OF WHICH GOT ME TO THINKING ABOUT THE LAST *CLUE* ON THE ANIMAL QUIZ!
I COULDN'T BELIEVE I'D ALMOST *FALLEN* FOR IT!

AFTER ALL THESE CONTROLLED ENVIRONMENTS, I NEEDED TO GET MY FEET BACK ON SOME REAL RIVER HEIGHTS GROUND.
AFTER ALL, SOMEONE WAS DEFINITELY SABOTAGING THE DOMES...
ANIMAL INFIRMARY
...AND WITH MALACHI CRAVEN IN JAIL DURING THE TRASHING OF THE ARCTIC DOME, IT WAS OBVIOUSLY NOT HIM.
CHIEF McGINNIS, PLEASE.

THE NEXT DAY I PAID A VISIT TO CHERI GOALE'S ESTATE.
THE GOALE ESTATE

HER HOME WAS LIKE A STATELY ENGLISH MANOR YOU'D SEE IN A MOVIE--EXCEPT THERE WAS NO MR. DARCY.

THANKS FOR SEEING ME, MS. GOALE! THIS PLACE IS REALLY ***SOMETHING***!
GLAD TO HAVE YOU, NANCY! AND I ***LIKE*** YOUR HYBRID CAR!

YES.

MY **GRANDFATHER**, MARTIN GOALE, BUILT THIS HOUSE. HE WAS AN INDUSTRIALIST WHO BECAME VERY RICH IN THE EARLY PART OF THE TWENTIETH CENTURY.

MONEY WAS HIS GOD.

HE CARED **NOTHING** FOR THE RIVERS AND SKIES HE *DESTROYED* FOR THE COMING GENERATION.

HE CARED **NOTHING** FOR HIS OWN CHILDREN AND GRAND-CHILDREN.

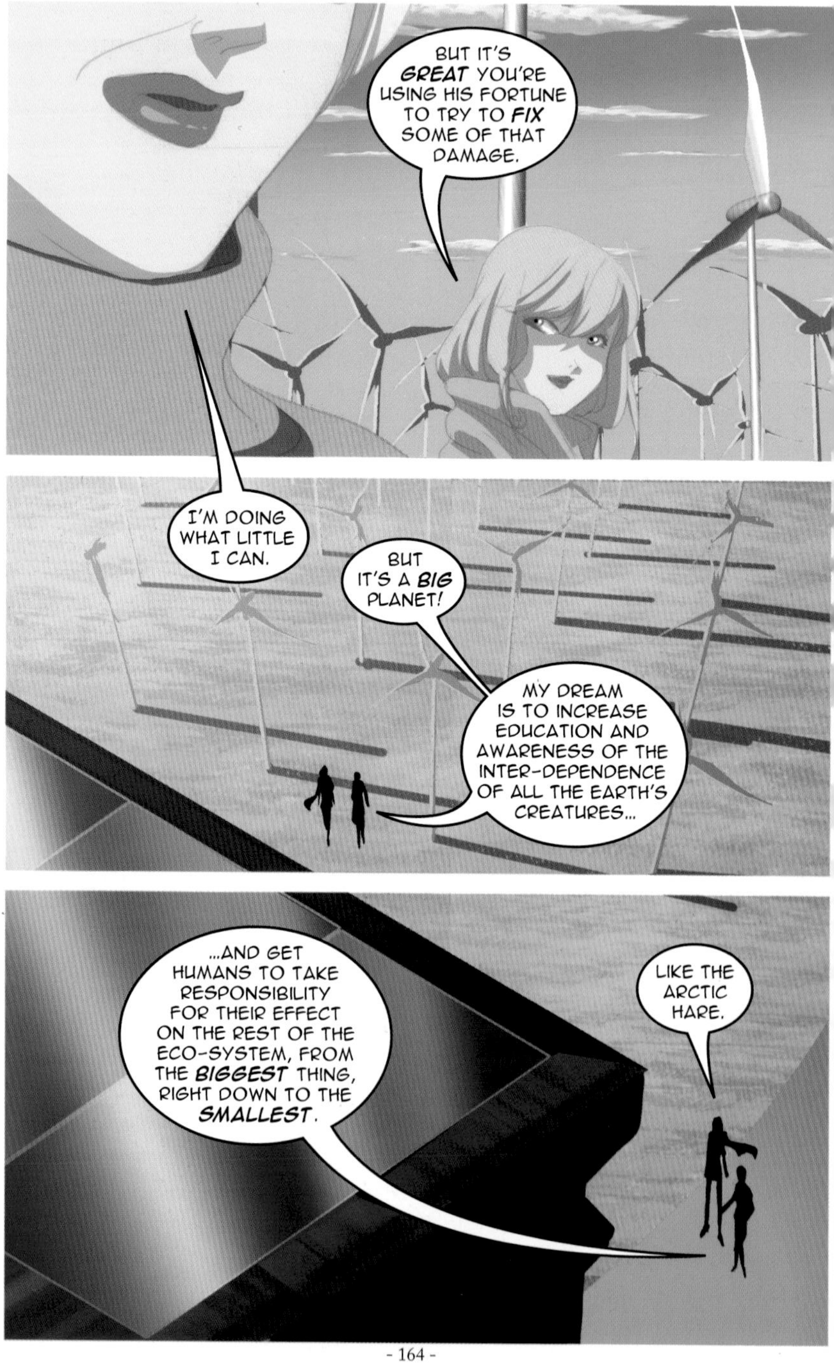

BUT IT'S *GREAT* YOU'RE USING HIS FORTUNE TO TRY TO *FIX* SOME OF THAT DAMAGE.

I'M DOING WHAT LITTLE I CAN.

BUT IT'S A *BIG* PLANET!

MY DREAM IS TO INCREASE EDUCATION AND AWARENESS OF THE INTER-DEPENDENCE OF ALL THE EARTH'S CREATURES...

EXACTLY!

SO, THESE SWIMMING AND TRACK TROPHIES ARE YOUR SON'S, RIGHT? I READ ABOUT HIS ATHLETIC ACHIEVEMENTS ON YOUR WEBSITE.

YES. DWAYNE SEEMS SO INTELLECTUAL, BUT HE'S ACTUALLY *QUITE* THE ATHLETE.

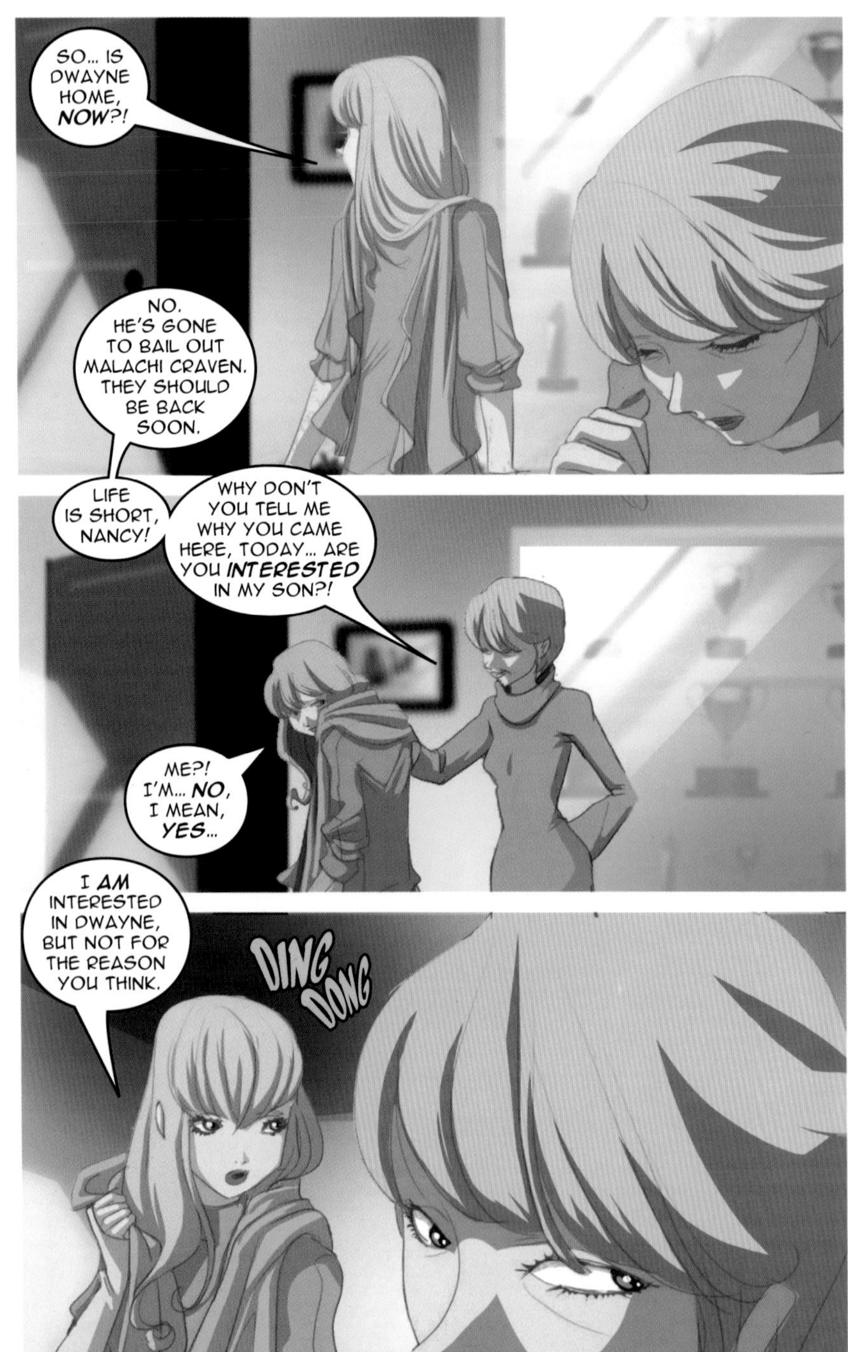
SO... IS DWAYNE HOME, NOW?!
NO. HE'S GONE TO BAIL OUT MALACHI CRAVEN. THEY SHOULD BE BACK SOON.
LIFE IS SHORT, NANCY!
WHY DON'T YOU TELL ME WHY YOU CAME HERE, TODAY... ARE YOU INTERESTED IN MY SON?!
ME?! I'M... NO, I MEAN, YES...
I AM INTERESTED IN DWAYNE, BUT NOT FOR THE REASON YOU THINK.
DING DONG

CHIEF McGINNIS! WHAT BRINGS *YOU* HERE? IS THERE NEWS?!
WELL, YES. IN FACT NANCY DREW ASKED ME TO MEET HER HERE.

NANCY HAS A THEORY I'D LIKE TO FOLLOW UP.
A THEORY?! ABOUT THE SABOTAGE?

MS. GOALE, I HAVE A WARRANT TO SEARCH THE HOUSE, SPECIFICALLY, YOUR SON'S ROOM.
DWAYNE?! HE HAS *NOTHING* TO HIDE!

IF THAT'S TRUE, THEN THIS WILL BE QUICK AND I'LL BE OUT OF YOUR WAY. DO YOU KNOW WHAT HE KEEPS IN THE CLOSET?
NO. I *NEVER* COME IN HERE UNASKED. I RESPECT HIS PRIVACY!

I'M SORRY ABOUT THIS. I REALLY AM...
CREEAAK

...BUT, LAST NIGHT *DWAYNE* SABOTAGED THE ARCTIC DOME. LUCKILY, NO ONE WAS HURT.

WHAT'S GOING ON?! WHAT ARE YOU ALL DOING IN MY ROOM? YOU CAN'T JUST COME IN AND...
MAYBE I SHOULD WAIT OUTSIDE?
YOU SHOULD STAY, MR. CRAVEN. SEEMS WE HAVE A PROBLEM, MR. GOALE... A **WARDROBE** PROBLEM.

DWAYNE, WHY?

I ***HAD*** TO, MOTHER!
HAD TO? THAT DOESN'T MAKE ***SENSE***! YOU WERE AS COMMITTED TO THE PARK AS SHE IS.

"DR. CRAVEN DISCOVERED THAT THE HYDRAULIC SYSTEMS OF THE BIODOMES USED OLD OILS THAT CONTAINED PCBs, A DANGEROUS, ILLEGAL CHEMICAL."
"AND THAT THE PCBs WERE LEECHING INTO THE RIVER WATER."
I WANTED TO FIX IT, BUT IT WOULD HAVE REQUIRED REMOVING THE ANIMALS AND DISASSEMBLING THE DOMES.
DENKLE, FEARING THE COST, GOT THE BOARD OF DIRECTORS OF THE GOALE CORPORATION TO OVERRULE ME.
AND SHE WAS BOUND BY AGREEMENT NOT TO DISCUSS THE PARK'S WORKINGS WITH ANYONE!
HER HANDS LEGALLY TIED, MY MOTHER BIT HER LIP, BUT I COULD SEE IT WAS KILLING HER INSIDE.
I THOUGHT THE ONLY WAY TO STOP THE POLLUTION AND SAVE HER REPUTATION WAS SABOTAGE!

BUT, WHY THE COSTUMES?!
***OKALA KANE*** MUST HAVE BROUGHT BACK MEMORIES FOR YOU, DR. CRAVEN.
YES, AND NOT VERY ***GOOD*** ONES!

I THOUGHT USING THE MYTHIC CHARACTERS WOULD DRAW ATTENTION, GET THE ***PRESS*** TO INVESTIGATE!
BUT, DENKLE RUINED THAT AS WELL BY CLAMPING DOWN ON ANY PUBLICITY!

CHERI AGREED TO COVER RECONSTRUCTION COSTS IF THE BOARD DECIDED NOT TO PRESS CHARGES AGAINST DWAYNE. SINCE THEY USED PCBs UNKNOWINGLY, ANY EMBARRASSING POLLUTION CHARGES WERE ALSO ***DROPPED***.

WELL, NOT ***ALL***, THE COMPANY THAT PROVIDED THE ILLEGAL HYDRAULIC OIL HAD A LOT TO ANSWER FOR!

NANCY, I MUST THANK YOU FOR HELPING ME IN SPITE OF OUR HISTORY. IF THERE'S ANYTHING I CAN DO FOR YOU...

THERE IS! TELL US THE ANSWER TO THIS LAST CLUE! "WHAT'S THE ONLY NATURAL ENEMY OF THE POLAR BEAR?"

WE'RE GOING CRAZY TRYING TO FIGURE OUT WHAT COULD BE SO ***BIG*** AND ***SCARY***!

# WATCH OUT FOR PAPERCUTZ

Hi, mystery-lovers! Welcome to the fourth double-dose of NANCY DREW DIARIES from Papercutz, those hearty boys dedicated to publishing great graphic novels for all ages. I'm Jim Salicrup, the Editor-in-Chief and honorary Snoop Sister.

Like the previous volume of NANCY DREW DIARIES, we're re-presenting a couple of classic NANCY DREW GIRL DETECTIVE graphic novels by Stefan Petrucha, Vaughn Ross, and Sho Murase. This time around we're presenting Vaughn's second and final Nancy Drew story that he illustrated. All further NANCY DREW DIARIES are illustrated by Sho, who clearly has a lot of affection for Nancy, Bess, and George. In fact, looking back on the story she illustrated here, I remember having to ask Sho not to dress the girls so lavishly—they look like they just stepped off the runways at New York City's Fashion Week. While it was perfectly in character for Bess to look all glam, it wasn't for Nancy and George. For Nancy, clothes are just something we're all required to wear, and she will dress appropriately for every situation, even if she can be a little absent-minded about such things. George, is virtually the opposite of Bess, and tends to dress like a tomboy. Let's just assume, that in "Global Warming," Nancy and George finally indulged Bess and let her pick out their outfits, shall we?

In this crazy transmedia world in which we live, I'd like to point out another interesting factoid regarding "Global Warning." It featured a character who first appeared in the Her Interactive PC game, Nancy Drew #15 "The Creature of Kapu Cave"—Malachi Craven. The folks at Her Interactive have been creating sensational Nancy Drew games for some time, and now you can find their latest games, such as *Nancy Drew: Ghost of Thorton Hall* available at the iPad App Store. "The Creature at Kapu Cave" is also still available here: http://www.herinteractive.com/shop-games/nancy-drew-the-creature-of-kapu-cave/. If you're enjoying this graphic novel in digital form, you can now buy and download the game right now! Imagine that—comics and games, now on the same device! (Don't worry, Non-techies—both are still available as books and discs, respectively.)

Stan Goldberg and Sarah Kinney, the NANCY DREW AND THE CLUE CREW graphic novel creators.

Also in "Global Warning," Nancy has a close encounter with a Komodo Dragon. While it's no big surprise that Nancy Drew seems to know all there is to know about almost everything, I like to think she first learned about such creatures back when she was much younger and took a bearded dragon home from school for a weekend. The full story behind that adventure can be found in NANCY DREW AND THE CLUE CREW #3 "Enter the Dragon Mystery," still available at booksellers and as an e-book. It was written by Sarah Kinney and was wonderfully illustrated by Stan Goldberg. Stan, winner of the Gold Key Hall of Fame award from the National Cartoonists Society, was a legendary comicbook artist, having colored most early 60s Marvel Comics and having drawn Archie and the rest of the Riverdale gang for over 35 years at Archie Comics. Unfortunately, Stan passed away on August 31st, 2014, and we miss him dearly. It was a really big deal for us to have an artist of Stan's stature work for us—someone whose work was ideally suited for comics for all ages—and we were greatly honored to be able to publish his work.

Coming up next in NANCY DREW DIARIES #5, "Ghost in the Machinery" and "The Disoriented Express," the first two of three stories that tie together, yet each is a complete story on its own. You don't want to miss it!

Thanks,

Jim

## STAY IN TOUCH!


| | |
|---|---|
| EMAIL: | salicrup@papercutz.com |
| WEB: | papercutz.com |
| TWITTER: | @papercutzgn |
| FACEBOOK: | PAPERCUTZGRAPHICNOVELS |
| REGULAR MAIL: | Papercutz, 160 Broadway, Suite 700, East Wing, New York, NY 10038 |

# NANCY DREW GRAPHIC NOVELS AVAILABLE FROM PAPERCUTZ

NANCY DREW AND THE CLUE CREW #1 "Small Volcanoes"

NANCY DREW AND THE CLUE CREW #2 "Secret Sand Sleuths"

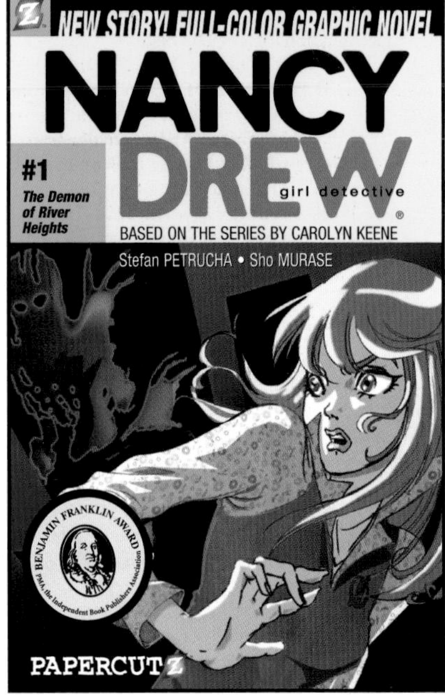


#1 "The Demon of River Heights"

NANCY DREW AND THE CLUE CREW #3 "Enter the Dragon Mystery"

#2 "Writ in Stone"

#3 "The Haunted Dollhouse"

#4 "The Girl Who Wasn't There"

#5 "The Fake Heir"

#6 "Mr. Cheeters Is Missing"

#7 "The Charmed Bracelet"

#8 "Global Warning"

#9 "Ghost In The Machinery"

#10 "The Disoriented Express"

#11 "Monkey Wrench Blues"